Woman in the Pillory

Woman in the Pillory

BRIGITTE REIMANN

Translated from German by Lucy Jones

PENGUIN BOOKS

PENGUIN INTERNATIONAL WRITERS

UK | USA | Canada | Ireland | Australia
India | New Zealand | South Africa

Penguin International Writers is part of the Penguin Random House group of companies
whose addresses can be found at global.penguinrandomhouse.com.

Penguin Random House UK
One Embassy Gardens, 8 Viaduct Gardens, London SW11 7BW

penguin.co.uk

Originally published as *Die Frau am Pranger* (Verlag Neues Leben, 1956)
This translation published in Great Britain by Penguin International Writers 2025

Text © Aufbau Verlage GmbH & Co. KG, Berlin, 1956, 2018
English language translation © Lucy Jones, 2025
001

The moral rights of the author and translator have been asserted

No part of this book may be used or reproduced in any manner for the
purpose of training artificial intelligence technologies or systems. In accordance
with Article 4(3) of the DSM Directive 2019/790, Penguin Random House
expressly reserves this work from the text and data mining exception.

Set in 11/13 pt Dante MT Std
Typeset by Six Red Marbles UK, Thetford, Norfolk
Printed and bound in Great Britain by Clays Ltd, Elcograf S.p.A.

The authorized representative in the EEA is Penguin Random House Ireland,
Morrison Chambers, 32 Nassau Street, Dublin D02 YH68

A CIP catalogue record for this book is available from the British Library

ISBN: 978–0–241–71897–1

Penguin Random House is committed to a sustainable future
for our business, our readers and our planet. This book is made from
Forest Stewardship Council® certified paper.

Woman in the Pillory

I.

Whenever she went along the village road, it looked as if she were walking through cold, autumn drizzle: her head hung low, her back was hunched, and her slight body shivered. She was in her late twenties and had been married for over five years, but strangers could have taken her for a nineteen-year-old.

She stood under the arch of the gate and stared at the telegram. '. . . three days' home leave . . .' Three days. She shivered more violently and seemed to grow slighter and more cowered. She went into the house, her feet dragging as usual, and put the telegram on the kitchen table.

'Heinrich's coming.'

Her sister-in-law was sitting in front of a plate of potatoes boiled in their skins, elbows on the table. She glanced up and said with a deep sigh, 'About time too. He can make sure that everything's in order, especially now. We won't get the spring tilling done without a man around here.'

'Just three days,' said the young woman. *Three days*, she thought fearfully, *three never-ending days and nights . . .*

The older woman shoved a potato into her mouth. 'Right.' She stood up, a strapping woman, hefty, with broad hips and brawny arms, almost a head taller than her brother's wife. She wiped her hands on her apron. 'He'll help out, Heinrich will, somehow. I'm sure he will.' She picked up the full milk churns from the bench like they weighed nothing. As she was going out of the door, she added, 'Make sure there's something decent on the table tonight for when Heinrich comes—'

He came. When he was standing on the threshold, the huge, heavyset man in his dun-grey uniform with a lance-corporal's chevron on his sleeve looked as if he would break the doorframe.

His sister clasped her hands around his neck, then stroked the silver chevron. 'You're a lance-corporal now! Done us proud, you have . . .'

He looked over her shoulder into the kitchen.

'Kathrin!'

The young woman was standing by the table, her shoulders sagging. When he put his arms around her, she started crying.

'Come, come . . .' He patted her back. 'There now . . .'

The young woman wept. He growled sympathetically at first, then impatiently, pushing her away. Her tears left damp stains on his tunic.

'Why the tears? Has something happened? Aren't you happy to see me?'

She wiped her sleeve across her face and swallowed. 'Of course I am, Heinrich.'

He sat down at the table, splaying his legs out, and dug in like a starving man.

'Home cooking's the best.'

Small droplets of sweat clung to his forehead.

Kathrin sat perched between the brother and sister, crushed by their warm, bulky flesh, their loud remarks and ripostes, and her husband's raucous laughter.

Her gaze lingered on his face. It was well-proportioned,

broad, with full lips and a fleshy nose, and brown eyes under gleaming, dark hair. In the village, the women called him Handsome Heinrich. When he'd run after Kathrin Laws, they'd looked her up and down in disapproval. No one understood what he saw in her, she herself least of all. She was a bland, ridiculously reedy wisp of a thing, and everything about her was pale – her hair, her face, even her eyes. She had none of the spit and grit of the other girls in the village. Yet he'd picked her out, along with the old Laws' acres of farmland, which enlarged his own plot by more than a third.

Now he was sitting at the table in his dun-grey uniform, chewing and chomping, guffawing and jawing.

'A strange bunch, those Russians are,' he was saying, 'sly and dangerous, the lot of 'em. We were marching into a village recently . . .'

How could she have imagined he'd have changed in the six or seven months since his last leave? Had she expected him to be less loud, big and strong?

'. . . and shots rang out from a farmhouse,' he continued. 'Then – peng! Our lieutenant was a goner. Partisans, of course.'

'My God, they're like animals,' Frieda said. 'Not proper people at all. The whole lot should have been strung up!'

'That's what we did,' Heinrich said, agreeably. 'But they're tough, a stubborn lot – they didn't make a peep. They spit in your face even when the noose is already around their necks.'

The young woman sat there listening, her eyes wide in shock, her face paler than usual.

He thumped her hand good-naturedly.

'That's just the way war is. You have to crack down

hard on them. And Russians are different from us, only half-human, get it?'

Kathrin kept her mouth shut, as she had done for years, no matter what the brother and sister thought or talked about.

That night, when she was finally released from his violent embrace, she cried in shame and fear. He was lying on his back, mouth half-open, snoring with a full belly and in rude health. And for the first time in those five years of cowering obedience, alongside her usual aversion and deference, a tiny ember of hatred glowed.

The next day she avoided him. She needn't have bothered because he ignored and talked over her anyway, like he'd done in all the years before he'd become a soldier. His crude jokes echoed through the house and farm, accompanied by approving laughter from his sister. The siblings strode about the stables and barns. He slapped his sister's backside. What a capable woman she was, keeping the place in order, just the way it should be.

While she was happy to bask in his praise, Frieda began grouching: they needed a man about the place, otherwise, they wouldn't manage the tilling in spring. She was no longer in her prime, after all. 'I'm going to rack and ruin behind the plough, and it's not like Kathrin can be relied on, that tiny scrap!'

Heinrich stuck up for his wife. 'She's not strong. She can't help that. You're right, though, you need a man around here.' He thought for a moment. 'Perhaps I can get you a prisoner of war to help out.'

Frieda raised her hands in protest. 'I'm not having a Russian here on the farm!'

'You aren't afraid, are you?' he asked, laughing. 'He

wouldn't come into the house. He'd sleep in the barn, and his upkeep wouldn't cost much. But you need a man around the place, Frieda.'

Ignoring her protests, he went to the local farmers' overseer, a man installed by the Reich Food Estate to supervise forced labour and grain supplies to the front. When he came back, he looked satisfied. 'They're going to allocate you a Russian next week.'

The two women sat in silence, the younger one hunched over with her hands in her lap, and a desperate expression on the coarse face of the older one.

Heinrich tried cajoling them. 'What's the big deal with some Russki? You'll manage him, no problem. Won't cost a thing, and the work will get done. That's the main thing!'

'It's not right, having to take one of them into our house!' complained Frieda. 'This bloody war!'

When she caught the look in her brother's eyes, she shrank back.

'You have the nerve to say *that* – you, a German woman?' He stood in front of her, feet planted wide apart. 'We know why we're fighting our war. And you're moaning about a filthy Russian? Don't make a fool of yourself, Frieda! A sturdy lass like you! Afraid of a Russki! It breaks my heart to see my lovely fields going to waste . . .'

She couldn't have looked more remorseful. All contrite and snivelly, she promised not to let him down. Then she tried to cheer herself up. 'They're only half-human, aren't they, Heinrich? And we could start on the field up at Hornberg at last . . .' She talked too much and too quickly, flapping about as she tried to appease her brother. Three or four others in the village already had prisoners, didn't they? They were easy to get along with, placid and knew how to work hard. 'None of them have caused a riot yet, and if you keep a firm hand on them, they can be put to good use.'

And so, it was decided.

On the third day, Heinrich Marten set off back to the front. The women accompanied him to the main town where the station was. When the train pulled in, his sister clasped her hands around his neck, snuffling and sobbing. His wife, thin, blonde and shivering, stood staring up at the carriage window, with the grey March sky overhead. She raised a hand hesitantly, as if forced, while Frieda next to her flapped a huge white handkerchief.

That's how they stayed in Heinrich's mind: his young wife, who seemed even slighter and paler next to his large, red-faced sister, one with her hand half raised, the other waving a handkerchief.

As the train pulled away eastwards, the two women walked the few kilometres back to the village and didn't say a word to each other.

2.

A few days later, Horst Lange, the local farmers' overseer, personally brought them a POW. While Frieda Marten bargained with Lange in the kitchen, the prisoner stood lifelessly in the yard, bundle in hand, staring at the ground with a dull gaze.

Kathrin pressed her face against the window and watched him, scared and curious.

The Russian was tall and broad-shouldered, his face simple and strong with sharp cheekbones and flat, dark eyebrows. Kathrin had seen Russians now and again. One had slanted eyes and Mongolian features, and she was afraid of him. Recently at the Meinhardt's farm, she'd had to go past him when he'd been forking manure and he'd glanced up at her as she'd clacked past in her wooden clogs. His dark eyes had only fixed on her for a moment, but she'd felt a deep jolt and had been dogged by a strange unease for days afterwards. She thought he was sure to have been the kind who raped women, killed children and sniped at German soldiers.

The prisoner in the yard raised his head as if he felt her watching him. She leapt back from the window, but for a few seconds, she'd glimpsed his eyes, set in a face that was thick with dirty stubble. Those eyes, so deep blue they were almost black, were set far apart in his grey face, and she realized that though she'd guessed him to be forty, he couldn't have been twenty-five.

By now, Frieda had sealed the deal with the farmers' overseer. 'Heil Hitler!' He left, and Frieda led the prisoner to the barn, where she showed him his place in the hayloft, which had a tiny hatch he couldn't wriggle through. The farmers' overseer had told her to lock the barn securely at night. If he did try to escape, the Russian wouldn't make it far, though: he barely spoke three words of German.

Kathrin had stayed in the kitchen and was standing by the oven, rearranging the pots and kettle, when Frieda came in. She didn't turn around when her sister-in-law said, 'His name's Alexei and he can barely string together three words of German.' She pointed to the slip of paper given to her by the overseer, and spelt out what it said: 'Alexei Ivanovich Luniev . . . funny, all Russians are called Ivan.'

'Where's he going to sleep?'

'Well, in the hayloft.'

They ate in silence.

Then the younger woman said abruptly, 'It's still so cold at night. Perhaps we should give him a blanket.'

The older woman looked up and inspected the other's face in surprise. 'Have you gone mad?'

'I just thought – I mean, he's going to freeze,' Kathrin mumbled.

'Then he can bed down in the hay.' Loudly and sharply, she added, 'They're our enemies. We can't coddle them in our blankets and give them God knows what for nowt in return. They shot at your husband! If you have a woollen blanket to spare, then send it to our men on the front, but don't give it to a Russian. Sometimes I think you're not right in the head!'

Kathrin had lowered her head and let the scoldings and accusations rain down on her without protest.

'Never heard such a thing!' Frieda's hand slammed onto the table. 'You don't seem to know where your loyalties lie – you, a German woman!'

Kathrin didn't dare answer back or think about how they still had to bring the prisoner his supper.

They ate quickly and in silence, while the Russian lay in the hay, freezing and hungry, listening to the evening wind squalling around the eaves. He wasn't sad or angry; he simply accepted this farm as one of many stops on the way to his final destination: Russia, victory and returning home.

And so, this was how POW Alexei Ivanovich Luniev arrived on the Martens' farm in 1943: placid, dirty and unshaven, with a scant bundle in his arms, not knowing when he would walk out of the gate for the last time.

3.

'Smooth as butter,' Frieda said, 'he's a dab hand.' She was peering through the kitchen window into the yard, where the prisoner was loading manure. One, two – he stuck the pitchfork in the pile; one, two – he flung a forkful onto the truck; one, two – his knees bounced in time, and the muscles on his arms and neck stood out.

The Russian put the pitchfork down, took off his cap and wiped his face and skull with the flat of his hand.

At the window, Kathrin cried out in shock: a blood-red scar the length of a finger ran across his shorn head.

'Grazed by a bullet, I expect,' her sister-in-law explained matter-of-factly, and then yelled out into the yard, 'Oi, you! *Pa-shol!*' She remembered this word from a storybook and shouted it at the Russian ten times a day. 'Get on with it, c'mon, *pa-shol!*'

For the first time, a farmhand was working on the Martens' land, and a Russian, to boot, who needed a firm hand and had to be prodded ten times a day – 'Get a move on, you, *pa-shol!*' – so that he'd get the work done – 'Chop, chop!' – whether it was loading manure, guiding the plough, milking the cows, feeding the pigs – 'Hey, *pa-shol!*' – as he ran back and forth to be in ten different places at once.

The man stuck his cap back onto his shorn head, grabbed the pitchfork and carried on loading the truck with manure – one, two, one, two – that he was supposed to drive out into the fields early next morning.

'A hardworking lad,' said Frieda. 'And quick and clever, there's that much to be said for him.'

'Maybe he's a farmer,' Kathrin said.

'Might well be.' Frieda heaved herself to her feet and rolled up her sleeves. 'People say they live like animals, with chickens and pigs in one room. And no wooden floorboards like we have, just dirt floors.' She took the milking pail from the bench. 'And they sleep on the stove – imagine that! On the stove!' She shuffled out of the kitchen in her wooden clogs across the yard to the cowshed, shouting back as she reached the door, 'Soak the laundry, Kathrin, d'you hear?'

'Yes, yes!' the younger woman shouted. Still watching the prisoner, she pulled the washtub out from under the windowsill in the corner.

The Russian carried on forking manure with an unperturbed air.

He'd been on the Martens' farm for a week already, and she hadn't said a word to him yet; all she'd done was watch him working from a distance, peering secretively out of the window down into the yard. Besides, orders in the house were given by her sister-in-law, who bossed Kathrin around as much as she did the Russian, glad she could run the place for her brother on the front who would find everything in order on his return: the house, stables and fields, and his wife and his sister too.

This was fine by Kathrin. She couldn't have brought herself to order around the stranger the way her sister-in-law did, and she couldn't have yelled '*Pa-shol!*' or 'Hey you, get a move on!' for anything in the world. She gave him a wide berth.

Kathrin took the washtub and hauled it over to the water pump in the yard. The water shot into the tin container. She bent down to pick it up and carry it back into the house.

The tub wouldn't budge. Helplessly, she stood there, bent over, trying in vain to lift it. Then she straightened up, red and hot. All at once, the Russian was next to her; he gently pushed her to one side, effortlessly picked up the heavy tub and carried it into the house.

Kathrin followed him and stood in the doorway while the young man put down the tub, saying quietly as he turned around:

'Thank you so much, Alexei.'

He looked at her and, for a moment, the apathy and stoicism vanished from his face. He smiled.

Confused and shocked, not knowing where to look, Kathrin quickly turned away. The man left, and she could hear his footsteps on the flagstones in the entrance hall alongside the hammering of her heart.

Her shoulders sagged forward.

She leaned on the doorpost and listened to the sounds of the evening. The Russian was singing. Kathrin hadn't sung for a long time, not since she was a little girl. But ever since she'd moved to this house, she'd fallen silent.

In the yard, the stranger's song was dark, mournful. It seemed both familiar and unfamiliar to Kathrin at the same time.

How he'd smiled ... For a few moments, his face had looked quite young again ... 'Thank you so much, Alexei.' What was the big deal? Just words said five to ten times a day, a throwaway phrase for a helping hand or a kind gesture. What was so special about what she'd said? A trivial phrase, probably something he'd only just about understood, and his name.

'Thank you so much, Alexei.' And at once she realized that in the seven days since the prisoner had arrived on their farm, her sister-in-law had only ever referred to him as 'the Russki' or, at best, 'the Russian'. She never called him by his name and only addressed him in sign language or with '*pa-shol!*', as if she were calling out 'giddy up!' to a horse.

Suddenly his singing stopped. Clogs clattered across the stones, and there was no sound in the dusk light except for the cows lowing and the rattling of their chains.

Kathrin hastily tucked a wisp of her hair under her dark headscarf, then bent down and piled the waiting laundry into the tub. When her sister-in-law checked on her, she found Kathrin silent and busy.

Frieda piled potatoes on a dish, dashing them with a stingy portion of onion and bacon gravy.

Without looking up, Kathrin said, 'He put his back into it today.'

'Well, so what?' bellowed Frieda, about to take the dish out.

With her head still lowered, Kathrin insisted, 'He's hard-working. The man should get a decent meal if he's supposed to work.'

'Well, so what?' Frieda thundered, quite a bit louder this time, but she stopped at the door.

With a firmness that was out of character, Kathrin said, 'A piece of bread and dripping won't make us any poorer. We can afford it.'

Maybe those last words clinched it: 'The Martens can afford to let their farmhand eat his fill, yes, they can still manage that!' Or maybe Frieda's good nature was stronger than her mock sternness after all – 'Well, true, he's certainly earned it.' Whatever the case, she gave in over the piece of bread and dripping. As her sister-in-law walked over to the barn, Kathrin, not seriously believing she'd win the argument, was as proud of that piece of bread as she would have been of a major victory.

4.

Two days later, when Frieda was visiting the Weckerlings for an hour or so, Kathrin brought the Russian a blanket. She waited until dusk and then walked, pressed close against the wall, heart beating fast, to the barn. That night, her sister-in-law had locked the door earlier than usual.

Alexei sat up when he heard the key in the lock. The door opened falteringly and just a crack, only wide enough for Kathrin to slip through. Now she was standing in the dimly lit barn, waning daylight filtering through the gaps in the woodwork and the tiny hatch in the roof. She looked around indecisively, shocked by her own courage.

Hay rustled in the corner; Alexei had got up and stepped closer. He brushed hay stalks off his tunic.

The woman shrank back, holding out the blanket and saying, 'Here you are!'

The Russian seemed tall and dark in the barn. He looked at her, but his expression remained blank. He didn't seem to understand.

'Cold,' Kathrin said, adding more loudly as if he'd be able to understand her better, 'freezing,' as she slapped her arms around her body to show what she meant.

He took the blanket. '*Spasiba*,' he said, '*spasiba*.' And the woman, hearing the soft sound of his mother tongue for the first time, understood and felt strangely moved by his voice. She thought she saw a trace of happiness on his face, and at the same time, regret. Embarrassed, she looked down at the floor.

Silence.

The gate to the yard clattered shut. Kathrin started, then stood frozen to the spot, her face ashen.

In her wide-open eyes, the man read more than she could have told him in a thousand words – that she felt abject and desperate, and utterly terrified too.

And in those moments, as she locked eyes with the stranger, she felt that he understood all of this.

She went red. Then she spun around, slammed the door shut and locked it, dashed back to the house, past her sister-in-law's stare and questions and up to her room, where she undressed in haste and pulled the cover over her head. There she lay, knees pulled up, freezing and frightened. Her courage and joy had vanished, replaced by fear and agonizing self-blame.

What have you done? she thought. *He's an enemy of your people, a man who shoots at German soldiers and your husband . . . Don't make excuses for yourself. Pity? A German woman doesn't pity her enemies. They aren't proper people . . . A piece of bread and dripping? A blanket? They're no better off in Russia – they live like animals . . .*

But – he's helpful . . . Because he carried a washtub into the house once? Don't make a fool of yourself, Kathrin! But – Heinrich has never done a thing like that, or if so, then with a coarse joke that's harder to bear than your hard work and frailty.

Does that give you the right to ruin your honour? The honour of a German woman? If Heinrich knew . . .

What a world! she thought. *I can't tell what's right any more . . . if the man's cold, he needs a cover. And what kind of honour is it anyway if you can ruin it by giving someone a piece of bread?*

There she lay, knees drawn in, freezing and scared, agonizing and justifying herself, yet knowing she'd never be able to shout 'Pa-shol!' and 'Oi, you!' and that she'd do just the same tomorrow as she'd done today . . .

The scene the next day was worse than Kathrin had feared. Frieda raged, hurling insults at her, grouching and threatening to tell her brother. The young woman cried and had no defence except tears and confused stammerings about pity and pleas for forgiveness.

Alexei was harnessing the horse and could hear the screaming in the house and the young woman's sobs. His eyes dark with anger, he put the bit in the animal's mouth with trembling hands, and swung himself up onto the cart, still looking at the house. He shouted at the horse, thwacking the reins across its back so that it set off with a sharp jolt and pulled the rattling wagon through the gateway.

At midday, Frieda came up to the field. He'd worked as hard as three men. This calmed her rage; and so she let the Russian keep the blanket, grunting and dissatisfied, but also feeling that she'd shown herself to be very generous.

Kathrin said nothing when her sister-in-law forgave her graciously; she said nothing either throughout the accusations and warnings that followed. But when she was sitting on the bench in front of the house peeling potatoes, she hummed a little ditty to herself, a silly counting rhyme she'd often sung as a child and whose words she'd long since forgotten.

5.

Kathrin was leaning against the crossbar of the window, her chin resting on her folded hands, her pale face tinged with the red light rising on the horizon. The sun was coming up over the violet edge of the woods.

She placed her fingertips on her eyelids and felt the blood beneath her skin. For a few minutes, she was at peace, unafraid of anything. The cool morning through her window showed a section of the muddy village road, the brown beams of the church and the apple-green and pink sky above.

Fists hammered on her bedroom door that felt like heavy blows to the back of her head.

'Kathrin, hey, Kathrin! Are you ready? Some people can sleep all day . . .'

She hastily buttoned her smock. The sun stood still, already growing pale over the woods, which sank back into the shadows and silence, blue and cool.

The Russian was washing himself under the pump in the yard. An ice-blue jet of water shot across his head and neck, colouring them crab-red. Kathrin, her head turned away, tried to walk past. As she did, Alexei straightened up. Dripping wet, his red, fresh face gleamed just like his dark blue eyes. He gave her a nod. She nodded back furtively, and a jolt went through her as if she'd been caught doing something wicked; she glanced back over her shoulder at the house and walked past him, shivering at the thought that her sister-in-law might have spotted their greeting.

She squatted on the milking stool, her head pressed against the cow's flank. A shadow fell across her. She looked up to see the Russian standing in the doorway. A single ray of pale sun flitted across his shaven skull, on which a golden fuzz was starting to grow back, as short as the feathers of a baby bird.

His hair's growing back, she thought and was surprised at the trace of relief she felt. He looked very different now, shaven and freshly washed, than when he'd stood in the yard for the first time. *How many days had passed since then? Let's see – twenty days, almost three weeks. Only three weeks?* she realized with surprise.

The Russian threw down hay for the three cows and the calf.

Kathrin picked up two full pails of milk and set them down by the cowshed door.

She hesitated.

The Russian clasped the young calf's muzzle with his broad hand.

He turned around.

Then he was next to her, picking up the two pails.

Kathrin went ahead. Alexei followed, balancing the buckets of foamy white milk. His gaze took in the woman's rounded back and her sunken head, her hair tucked away in an ugly cotton scarf. *Kathrin*, he thought, *Katja*.

As if she could feel his gaze, she sped up and instinctively straightened her back. All at once, she felt ashamed of her stained apron and the dark headscarf pulled down over her hairline, as severely as a nun's coif.

She almost ran the last steps to the farmhouse door, so that her heavy black woollen skirt thrashed against her legs.

Kathrin had never paid much attention to what she wore; she'd never enjoyed wearing pretty clothes.

Who for anyway? she thought as she stood in front of the mirror in her room with the walnut wood frame that cut off the reflection of her thin body from the hips down.

Who for anyway? she wondered as she slipped off her skirt and the bodice with sweat stains under the arms. She avoided looking in the mirror while she changed.

She pulled on a light, grey cloth skirt, painstakingly choosing a blouse from the three or four she owned. In the very bottom drawer, she found a colourful sweater she'd knitted two years earlier from odds and ends of wool, with red, green, blue, yellow and brown stripes. She'd worn it only once and never again because it had seemed too colourful and showy.

Now, standing in front of the mirror, she liked it even though, being tight, it accentuated her chest more than the loose blouses and jackets she usually wore.

Even after five years of marriage, Kathrin was still as self-conscious as a young girl. Now in the mirror, for the first time, she admired her breasts and hips, and her wrists, which were too long and delicate for her rough hands and splintered nails.

She skipped down the stairs and ran like a young girl across the yard, her grey skirt swinging in a pleasant arc around her legs.

At that moment, Alexei was leading the horse out of the stable.

Kathrin patted the warm, silky brown animal's neck, which tautened under her hand. She blew into its nostrils and laughed. The Russian stood there, surprised by her graceful transformation. Her eyes were shining.

The horse snorted and ran its muzzle over her shoulder. She flinched. Alexei laughed, grabbed the horse's mane and gently stroked it. Kathrin looked at him and when he nodded at her, she gave him the ghost of a smile.

'My God, what are you dawdling for *this* time?' Frieda cried out. Then Kathrin ran off in haste, her head lowered, leaving behind the clatter of hooves on the stones and the Russian's silent anger.

Frieda, her brawny hands on her hips, launched into a torrent of abuse and accusations. Where had she been all this time? Did she think elves would do the housework? 'And in your finest get-up, so early in the morning! Think you're a princess now, do you?'

Kathrin stood up for herself. She had to go into town to do the shopping and – the thought came to her that instant – 'I was going to drop by the Meinhardts. Trude has a good recipe for steamed dumplings.'

The Mongolian prisoner of war with the dark eyes worked on Meinhardt's farm. Frieda had never caught sight of him or seen his troubling eyes. She would understand why Kathrin was interested in a recipe, but never why she might be interested in a stranger from Asia.

Relieved, Kathrin slipped back into the house behind her sister-in-law's broad back. She hadn't yet found the string bag when she heard Frieda's coarse voice belting across the yard again, as she ordered the Russian to harness the horse – 'You, *pa-shol!*'

She waited until she heard the cart rattling through the gateway. Then she left too. She was ashamed of the weakness she'd shown the Russian, and of being so obedient and afraid. She couldn't have brought herself to stand next to her sister-in-law and watch the Russian harnessing the horse as if she were like her – a loud, harsh woman who lorded over land, animals and people.

Kathrin walked along the road. She picked her way unsteadily between the muddy brown puddles filled with murky rainwater, moving with the same shy caution she always felt when she knew other people were looking.

She said hello to a couple of schoolboys with satchels; she said hello to a farmer's wife with a baking tray under her arm; she said hello to an old farmer who was sitting up on his cart and returned her greeting by tipping his hat with his whip handle. She said hello left and right, walking past with her head lowered, but she didn't stop to talk to anyone.

The village womenfolk were used to her. The Marten girl's a quiet sort, a mysterious one, they said. She can't have it easy with Frieda – that woman had a mouth on her like a foghorn and could swear like the best of them.

Kathrin knew what they said about her and that the more reserved she was, the more they gossiped. When she saw two women standing in front of the inn, putting their heads together as she approached, she ducked her head even more, trying to make herself even slighter, as if afraid they would laugh right in her face because she was different from them. They were fully in charge, whereas she, as everyone in the village knew, was no more than a maid on her own farm, ordered around by her sister-in-law, with no say whatsoever. Even though she was the mistress of the house! She'd just handed over her inheritance to her husband when they married, as easily as that. Dear-oh-dear-oh-dear, that young Marten girl was a fool!

A new, keener fear now rose in her next to the old, familiar one. The Martens had taken on a new farmhand, a POW . . . So why was Kathrin wearing a new skirt? Why did she have on that colourful pullover? Why did Kathrin stand in the yard in the mornings patting the horse's neck with the stranger standing beside her? Why did Kathrin laugh when the stranger was close by? Why did Kathrin sing when the stranger was working in the yard?

She ran on, away from the women's gazes. She ran past the inn and down the street to Trude Meinhardt's farm at the very edge of the village, where the bumpy road turned into an asphalted avenue and the first cherry trees lined both sides of the path.

Kathrin felt calmer as soon as the farm gate closed behind her. It was good and clean. Everything was good and clean at the Meinhardts' – the people, the house and the small garden out front, which was smothered in marigolds and delphiniums in the summer.

Never a loud or vulgar word was said in this place. The mistress of the house had suffered a great deal and this had settled on the farm and the people who lived on it.

Trude's fiancé had not come back from the First World War. The man she later married had been killed by a falling beam during a barn fire, and her eldest son had fallen on the Western Front three years ago.

So now only Trude's elderly father and her second son, a lad of thirteen, were left on the farm. Besides her farming work, Trude Meinhardt was also the district nurse, which was perhaps why she'd been one of the first villagers to be allocated a prisoner of war.

Kathrin found her in the small quarters that served as a sickroom, which was furnished with just a sofa covered in an oilcloth and a little vitrine in which medicine bottles and white bandages were kept.

Trude was just getting her son back on his feet; he'd been sitting on the sofa having his knee bandaged. The small, wiry, dark-haired lad bobbed up and down a little to test how tight the bandage was. Then he shook Kathrin's hand and said very formally, 'Good morning, Aunt Marten,' then left.

Trude straightened up. She was a tall, stout woman with a full bosom; her face was thin, severe and very pale, framed by ebony hair.

Without preamble, Kathrin asked, 'Does your Russian eat at your table?'

The woman's dark eyes fixed on Kathrin's face, without a trace of surprise.

Kathrin didn't lower her gaze. She waited.

'Of course he eats at our table. He works with us too, after all. He's a person, in the end, just like us.'

Kathrin sat down on the sofa, her knees pressed together like a young girl, her hands folded in her lap. She said, 'Frieda would never allow it.'

'No, Frieda wouldn't.'

Kathrin stood up. Then in a high voice, she quickly said, 'He's good to me. He helps in any way he can. We have to do something for him, too. We can't just yell *"Pa-shol!"* at him and bring his food to the barn. That's no way to treat anyone.'

Trude lay an arm around her shoulders. She said over her head, 'No, it's not, Kathrin.'

Then she suddenly pushed the young woman away and smiled.

'Your hair's nice, Kathrin.' She said it as if it were the only reason Kathrin had come to her. 'You should take care of it, wash it with camomile in the evenings, you know? That'll give it more sheen.'

Kathrin went red. 'Do you really think so?' she said hesitantly. Trude nodded. Both women left the room. At the door, they stopped at the same time and looked at one another. Kathrin leaned on the doorpost, her head back, feeling faint. *She knows everything*, she thought. Fear gripped her chest like a cold iron hoop, forcing a sharp intake of breath.

'Kathrin,' said Trude, 'no one can help you. You have to help yourself, you hear? You mustn't be afraid. Do what your heart tells you to. We're all people in the end. This war . . . listen to me, we all have to hang on tight to the little warmth we have left. Otherwise, we'll freeze to death.'

The prisoner was hunched over the gate, hammering in a post.

'Good morning,' Kathrin said.

'Good morning,' he replied, enunciating each syllable clearly.

'That's Muchtar,' Trude said. 'If I didn't have him on the farm, my crops would be ruined.' She turned to Muchtar who was now standing in front of her with his eyes lowered, but not submissively. 'Have you sorted the potatoes?'

'Yes, ma'am.'

Kathrin felt the pressure of Trude's hand on her shoulder; she was staring with a fixed gaze at the prisoner's face. A sharp crease appeared between her eyebrows. As if testing herself, she asked sternly, 'Do you speak German?'

The man nodded.

'Do all Russians speak German?' Kathrin asked.

'Many,' he said. 'Most of us. We learn it at school.' He spoke German with difficulty but clearly. Without moving his lips, he flashed a smile that vanished quickly, like a gust of wind across a dark lake.

Kathrin turned aside, feeling awkward. Once they were out on the road again, and she was squeezing Trude's hand goodbye, she said, 'Heinrich says that Asians are the worst.'

Trude laughed. 'Muchtar's a cattle breeder,' she said. 'They herd together in groups. In summer, they live in tents. It's hard to imagine – a very different kind of life. He doesn't talk much either.'

She nodded at Kathrin. 'You don't need an excuse to come over and see me, you know that.'

Kathrin walked back home up the village road, now upright with her shoulders thrown back. The sun glinted in the puddles.

'Well, where's the steamed dumplings recipe?' asked her sister-in-law.

Oh, why is she so rude! And why am I so afraid of her?

'Oh, I forgot it,' said Kathrin sheepishly.

'What? You went over to the Meinhardts' and forgot the recipe?' Frieda's outrage turned her ruddy complexion an even deeper shade of red.

Here we go again, thought Kathrin and sure enough, her sister-in-law started grouching about how Kathrin was a scatterbrain. 'Off you go, gallivanting about the village all morning, the work here's not done and—' She fell silent. Kathrin had started and was craning her neck, listening to the clatter of hooves in the yard.

Kathrin closed her eyes, and the hooves pounded their way through her head. *You mustn't be afraid, Kathrin.*

She opened her eyes and said coldly and calmly, 'People forget things sometimes. You don't need to start nagging straight away.'

Frieda's round, brown eyes grew even rounder in surprise. Kathrin said, 'Give me Alexei's food. I'll bring it to him, he'll be hungry.'

Frieda was speechless. In Kathrin's eyes, there was a new, dangerous glint.

The sister-in-law ladled soup without saying a word. Her face blazed, round and red with bewilderment and annoyance.

Kathrin carried the dish with both hands. For the first time, she brought the prisoner his food.

Alexei was sitting on the upturned trough next to the pump. He took the dish, and their fingertips brushed. Kathrin hastily pulled back her hand. The Russian lowered his head and ate quickly and heedlessly.

At that point, Kathrin should have left. But she didn't. Instead, she sat down on the pipe of the pump.

The farmers' overseer had said he could barely string three words of German together. But Kathrin knew better. Half-despondently, half-decisively, she thought: *I should ask him. Who'd have thought a question could be so hard* . . .

The April sun was already warm. In the gutter, sparrows were making a racket and in the gaps between the stones, hundreds of green, silky threads of young grass were sprouting.

Kathrin looked down at the Russian's hand using the spoon – a wide hand with nicely shaped nails and long fingers, the right kind to grip young animals during a birth. *He could have helped with the bull calf during that difficult delivery*, she thought.

Her fingers firmly grasped the smooth, cool iron of the water pipe.

'Alexei,' she said.

He lifted his head so suddenly, it was as if he'd been waiting for her to say his name or a word – any word. Sparks of sunlight danced in his pupils. Kathrin locked eyes with him as if transfixed by a blinding beam that had hit her out of the darkness.

'Do you speak German, Alexei?' she asked. Her voice was unnaturally high with excitement, as if something extremely important was about to be decided.

In seconds, the sparks in his eyes went out. He lowered his lids and his face took on the same dull, sealed expression of those first days in the yard when he'd looked at the ground, holding his meagre bundle.

He shrugged and murmured:

'I – nothing understand.'

Kathrin knew he was lying. She jumped up and ran

into the house, stopping at the foot of the stairs. She flung her head against the banister and sobbed.

Frieda appeared next to her before she could run up the stairs. The large woman put her arm around Kathrin's waist with unusual gentleness and asked in a shocked voice what was wrong. 'Was the Russki rude to you?' Kathrin shook her head vehemently. 'Are you worried about Heinrich because he hasn't written for so long?'

Kathrin looked up with such a perplexed, blank expression that had Frieda's mind not been on her brother the instant she said his name, she surely would have noticed. His name was like a slap in the face for Kathrin. *Oh God! There's someone else out there!* she thought. *Oh God, there's a man – my own husband – out there!* He hadn't written for weeks, but she hadn't missed his letters.

Kathrin started sobbing again, so wildly and desperately that Frieda, for whom there was no better or braver person in the world than her brother, imagined she was crying out of sheer worry for him. Very gently, she pulled Kathrin down onto the first stair and sat heavily next to her.

'Come, Kathrin, you mustn't cry,' she said, 'nothing will have happened – the post often takes a long time these days.' As she clumsily tried to comfort her, tears welled up in her own eyes.

As she felt the warmth of the woman close beside her and her strong arm around her waist, Kathrin's conscience pricked. She didn't deserve this, heaven knew, not this! She'd forgotten Heinrich who, by now, was maybe lying wounded, maybe dead, in the country of the other man who now worked on their farm. There she was in a colourful sweater while the letter was perhaps already on its way – '. . . fallen in the line of duty' – and then she'd be forced to wear a black widow's dress.

Now Kathrin began to comfort her sister-in-law with almost the same words as her, gently and clumsily. She silently vowed never to say 'Alexei' again, and never to ask 'Do you speak German?'

Frieda wiped her eyes with her blue checked handkerchief and said, 'This blasted war! And then this Russian on our farm! Here we are, thinking day and night about Heinrich, fretting and not sleeping – and then some Russki turns up, and I'd like nothing better than to send him packing. They're only to blame for this war and everything! The sooner we can do everything ourselves again, the better. Better to do it all myself and flog myself to death than—'

Kathrin sat up, saying quickly and loudly, 'We need him. He has to stay on the farm until—' She faltered, then added quietly, 'until Heinrich comes back.'

Until Heinrich comes back . . . then it'll all be over, she thought.

Heinrich Marten, striding across the farm again, tall, strong and healthy, his laugh reverberating around the house, his loud voice, and his strong arms around her.

Alexei was now just a name, a memory leaping out of the dark like a flash of light, shimmering sunspots in a droplet of water that vanished as quickly as the stirrings of life that began in her that day in March when he stood in the yard for the first time. Now everything was as grey and cold as it always was, and she would walk as if through cold autumn drizzle, shivering, her back hunched – for ever and ever.

In the following days, Kathrin slunk gloomily around the house, not saying much, keeping her distance from the stranger like she'd done in the first weeks. Sometimes in the morning when the sun rose over the edge of the woods, she stood at the window and cried without knowing why.

6.

The Russian Alexei Luniev was extremely agitated, but he couldn't work out why. When Frieda Marten let him out of the barn every morning, having locked him in overnight like an animal that might suddenly run away, he looked around as if hoping to find something he'd lost. But he never admitted to himself that he was looking for the other woman, or keeping an eye out for her pale face at the windows of the house. He had a feeling Kathrin was avoiding him with the same gentle resolve with which she'd previously sought him out.

One morning, when April was already drawing to an end, he entered the shed to give the cows water. There she was, squatting on the milking stool, hands in lap, her expression empty. Her eyes, which had dark rings around them, were sad and unusually large.

Kathrin spotted him. She wasn't startled; it was as if she'd been waiting for him. She said, 'Ach, Alexei,' in a tone that let the man know everything, without saying the thousands of words that burned in her heart. Now he had to walk the few paces that divided them. He brushed her hand. 'Kathrin,' he said. 'Katja.' She sat very still.

But the steps to cross all that divided them had not yet been taken. A name alone could not build a bridge.

Kathrin jumped up. She grabbed the milk pail and ran across the yard, leaning hard to one side under its weight.

Alexei made an involuntary movement as if to run after her. But he forced himself to stay put, one shoulder leaning against the doorpost.

He was quicker than the woman to realize what was happening, and it hurt him less because he was not chained to the village or the past, unlike her. As he stood in the cowshed of Martens' farm, watching the woman rush away, he understood that they would no longer avoid each other because they no longer could.

For the first time, he felt how deeply Kathrin's image had imprinted itself on his heart – her fear and kindness, helplessness and shyness, and her fight to stay firm and brave.

How could he have believed that overcast day in March when he'd stood here for the first time that this farm was just a stopover on the way to his final destination?

Alexei Luniev had such a deep-rooted faith in his country that he'd never doubted for a moment how the war that brought him here must end. But when would the end come? And what would happen to Kathrin when it did?

When I was fighting, he thought, *when I saw my burned-down village, when the damned Germans hauled me through their hellish camp, I always thought of my Ukraine, and our victory and returning home after the war . . .*

And now I think of Katja. When this war is over . . . what will happen to Katyusha?

Kathrin had run into the house, and it took all her self-control to hide her agitation from Frieda.

Then the letter from Heinrich Marten came. Frieda, who'd taken to standing in front of the gate at eleven in the morning to keep an eye out for the postman, grabbed the grey envelope from the old man's hands no sooner than he'd closed his postbag. She dashed into the kitchen. 'Heinrich's written!' Her cheeks glowed bright red, and her huge chest was heaving. 'Finally!' Tears were streaming down her face.

Kathrin took the letter. She ripped open the envelope and read, her mouth half-open. Her eyes raced across the lines, desperately searching for some comfort or a kind word.

His heavy, slanted handwriting was scrawled across the rough paper, the words spaced far apart. Heinrich reported that he was healthy, that he was well. He hadn't been able to write for a long time because conditions on the front were tense. They were constantly caught up in combat operations and were sometimes pushed back. 'But that doesn't mean anything!' he wrote. 'We'll be moving forwards soon, you'll see!' Kathrin's eyes sped over the lines, half-laughing, half-crying. Frieda gawped over her shoulder, avidly taking in each of her brother's words. Ach, Heinrich was alive, he was healthy, they were moving forwards . . .

Then, just a casual line: they'd tracked down partisans in a village, they'd smoked out the whole pack and lined the villagers against the wall – 'liquidated' was the name for it in this war.

Kathrin lowered the letter and had to sit down, her face as white as the wall. She closed her eyes. She saw machine guns ripping through the bodies of women and children . . .

Startled, Frieda grabbed the young woman's shoulders. 'My God, what's the matter, Kathrin? Do you feel sick?'

Kathrin opened her eyes. She was sitting in the kitchen of a German farmhouse. Outside the sun was shining and in the yard, the chickens were squawking. The fire in the hearth was crackling away under the kettle. Her sister-in-law's face swam into focus close to hers, but she heard her voice as if from far away.

'You do take everything to heart! That's just the way war is. I don't get you – just think of what the Russians are doing! Sniping at our men . . .'

Kathrin stared at Frieda's round, healthy face, appalled. She jumped to her feet, ran out of the kitchen, up the stairs into her room and locked the door. She threw herself onto the bed and sobbed, biting into the pillow. Murderers! Bloody murderers!

But then she straightened up and smoothed out the letter. *Read it to the end! All of it!* she thought.

She read: A mother holding a child had run over to the soldiers, a pale-faced blonde woman. God, he'd pitied her, but orders were orders!

God, he'd pitied her . . .

Mingling with Kathrin's feelings of deference and fear, a flame shot up from the tiny ember of hatred that had begun to glow inside her on the first night of his leave. It burned through everything that still bound her to this man – five years of marriage and joint ownership of a few hectares of farmland.

But there was one person for whom she could put right some of what the others were doing to his people. She didn't think for a moment that the Russian thought she was one of them. He must have known she had nothing to do with those wolves, the Nazis, and that she had nothing in common with the man whose name she'd taken.

Kathrin went back down to the kitchen and flung the letter into the fire. When her sister-in-law ticked her off – Had she gone completely mad? She hadn't finished reading it yet! – Kathrin turned around, looked her coldly up and down and said, 'It wasn't worth reading. The rest was just for me.' Then she carried on, 'From now on, Alexei will eat with us at the table.'

For several minutes, her sister-in-law sat in a stupor, not understanding. Then her face changed colour.

Kathrin leaned on the table. *You mustn't be afraid.* Her sister-in-law braced her arms on her ample hips and yelled, neck thrust forward, into Kathrin's face: 'You're not right in the head! Have you lost your mind completely? The Russki, eat at our table? Never, I tell you, never! Never! Not in my house! He's not setting foot in my house, d'you hear? Oh, just you try! What do you think Heinrich—'

With a forceful hand gesture, Kathrin cut off her sister-in-law mid-sentence. 'Whatever Heinrich has to say about it, I don't care.'

This took Frieda's breath away.

'Never!' she panted, beside herself with rage. 'Never, never!'

Kathrin said, 'I'm the head of the house, not you! You're only here on sufferance, you understand? For far too long you've been ordering me around – and now that's over, for good! I'm the one who's going to run things around here from now on and I say that the Russian eats at our table. If you don't like it, you can leave.'

The young woman stood upright, her head held high, and her sister-in-law realized that this was a new, changed Kathrin before her, the mistress of the house. Her mood snapped from anger to self-pity. She began to blubber and sat in a huddle at the table. 'This is how I'm thanked for everything I've done for this farm . . . Worked my fingers to the bone, and now this! All I do is fret day and night, and then you send me packing.'

Kathrin looked at her without pity. 'No one is sending you packing, Frieda. I just don't want you telling me what I can and can't do. I know very well. I'm not a small child and don't need your orders.'

Frieda lifted her head; her face was blotchy and swollen with tears.

'Kathrin,' she wailed, 'how can you treat me this way? All I ever wanted was the best for you . . .' And then, meekly, when she saw that her words were bouncing off Kathrin, she added, 'I won't interfere in your business any more. Do whatever you like, just' – at this, she became agitated again – 'just don't bring the Russki into the house. Kathrin, what will people in the village say—?'

'Many of them,' Kathrin interrupted, 'let their prisoners eat with them at the table. They work with us, after all. We'll stick to what I said.' Kathrin only knew that the Meinhardts let their prisoner in the house, but Frieda needed reassurance about what 'people' would say.

Kathrin left. Behind her, the gasps and sobs stopped as soon as she closed the door, replaced by the hush of eavesdropping.

Alexei was cleaning the plough on the threshing floor. As he squatted down to polish its blade, he quietly hummed a tune under his breath, a melancholy song. Kathrin lay a hand on his shoulder. He looked up.

She said, 'You speak German, Alexei. I know you do.

The Meinhardts' prisoner told me that most of you learn it at school. I won't tell anyone. You don't think I'd tell on you, do you? You understand what I'm saying, don't you?' She paused.

Alexei nodded.

'You don't need to be afraid, Alexei. I'm not afraid either. Things aren't as difficult as I always thought they were. You're going to eat with us at the table from now on.' She faltered. It sounded as if she were offering him a gift; that's not how she'd wanted it to seem. What had she wanted to say? Confused, she gave him a searching look. *You understand that it's not a gift, don't you? It's just how things should be.*

Slowly, the Russian said, 'Thank you, Kathrin.'

She heard his voice speaking German for the first time. It was a miracle, like a mute person suddenly gaining the power of speech.

She grasped his hand because she knew he'd understood – not just the words but what she hadn't put into language.

'Come,' she said.

In the kitchen, Kathrin laid the table, and Alexei put the plates out and lay spoons next to them.

Frieda's place remained empty.

The Russian stared silently at the bare plates, the unoccupied chair at the head of the table and then at Kathrin. She felt his accusation and, feeling ashamed, went in search of her sister-in-law.

She found Frieda up in her room, her round face screwed up in woe and anger. Kathrin would have liked nothing more than to leave her there where she was. But the Russian and his silent appeal were stronger than her desire for revenge, which she now felt ashamed of. Forcing herself to be kind towards her deeply offended sister-in-law, she coaxed and even apologized to Frieda, who, taking advantage of this unexpected concession, dug her heels in all the more.

But as Kathrin didn't want to return to the kitchen without Frieda, she used all her powers of persuasion. Not that she was very gifted in that way; she'd never been able to talk others into doing things – in fact she'd never even tried. So, she blundered about for a while until she finally induced Frieda to sit down at the table with the Russian.

Because she was used to giving orders, it cost Frieda the utmost effort to sit facing the prisoner and not to jump up and slam her fists on the table and shoo him out, the intruder. She ate in acrimonious silence, not once looking up from her plate, pretending that the stranger wasn't even there. She'd barely swallowed her last bite before she stood up and left.

Outside in the entrance hall, she shuffled about the milk churns while listening out to see if the pair of them in there were talking to each other.

But the kitchen was silent, and not long afterwards, the Russian came into the entrance hall too. When Frieda, in the mood for a fight, shoved past Alexei just when he was going out the door, he stood back politely and let her go first. Frieda turned and threw him a filthy look. The Russian's face was impassive, but his eyes contained an expression that made Frieda lower hers and hastily turn away.

Kathrin was standing in the kitchen and, as she washed the dishes, she sang songs that she hadn't sung since she was a girl.

In the evening, she washed her hair with camomile, just like Trude had told her.

'My God, you're turning into a vain one,' Frieda needled her.

As evenly as possible, Kathrin replied. 'My hair's like straw. I have to take care of it now and then. It's not like I can run into town just to go to the hairdresser.'

It wasn't until she'd wrung out her dripping wet hair and wrapped it in a towel that she dared look at her sister-in-law. There she sat, legs splayed, her hands folded across her stomach, watching the younger woman, her bottom lip thrust out.

'A-ha,' Frieda said deliberately after a long silence. 'You're taking care of your hair, and you can't just run to the hairdresser.' She added what she thought was a pregnant pause. 'And just tell me this, why do you make yourself so pretty, now of all times, hmm?'

She was being too obvious. Even someone less timid than Kathrin could have read her mind.

Kathrin turned to the drain and poured the water away, rinsing after it very carefully, taking as long as she needed for the shock to settle and to wipe all trace of it from her face.

Lie, Kathrin thought, *just tell a lie* . . . She'd often lied, mostly out of fear of being scolded for her clumsiness. Like many forced into humiliation and obedience, lying was the only way she could find some quiet to shut herself off from the noisy, hostile world around her. However, she'd never knowingly told a lie for her own selfish purposes; she wasn't a cunning person.

But faced with her sister-in-law's suspicions, her cunning grew, and her deviousness came naturally.

'Heinrich's always said I should wash my hair more often, with camomile, to give it a sheen. He's always admired Liesel Weckerling's plaits. I don't want my husband eyeing other women now, do I?' She laughed. 'And when he's home on leave again – oh, I'll make him stare. Don't you think?' She chattered on about Liesel Weckerling and Heinrich, saying any old thing. She sounded so sincere and looked so tender and joyful as she pretended to imagine her husband's surprise that even a woman less gullible than Frieda would have been taken in.

Oh, Kathrin knew very well how to put an end to her sister-in-law's suspicions. While the young woman rubbed her hair dry and brushed it, they gabbled about Heinrich.

Frieda found no end of virtues in him, praising his strength and prudence, and with a chuckle she told stories about his funny exploits. Even as a young lad . . .

At last, Kathrin was able to escape their torturous conversation. Up in her room, she stood in front of the mirror with the walnut frame, brushing her hair for half an hour until it fell loosely over the nape of her neck, and down to her shoulders.

Her face, framed by her pale-blonde hair that glinted red every time she moved her head in the dim lamplight, looked very young.

She inspected herself in the mirror, beginning to discover herself.

7.

A warm breeze drifted across the field. The soil broke into gleaming brown clods beneath the blade of the plough, and a bitter, aromatic smell of earth rose. The Russian was steering the plough, and the young woman was leading the horse, up and down the furrows, up and down.

In the distance, the church bells in the village struck twelve. Kathrin and Alexei sat down at the edge of the field and ate what the young woman had brought. She passed him the stone jug filled with coffee. Their hands touched, and Kathrin blushed but she didn't pull her hand away. Momentarily, her fingers stayed on the cool, brown jug next to his. But there was no intimacy in her smile.

When Alexei went to get up, Kathrin gestured for him to stay.

He stretched out in the grasses, his arms behind his neck, and squinted up into the silky blue, lofty sky over them.

Kathrin sat next to him, her hands folded over her knees, her skirt pulled tightly down below her ankles. She stole a look at his face.

'You're homesick, Alexei,' she said miserably.

The man turned to face her.

'Yes,' he said.

She lowered her eyes. *Of course*, she thought, *how could*

he not be? So far away from Russia and his village, his mother – and who knows who else he misses?

'You want to go home, don't you? You'd leave today if you could, right?'

'Yes,' he said quickly and loudly, but only to drown out the other voice that whispered: *No, not yet. Not today. Not right away.*

The pain that went through Kathrin was so sharp that the Russian felt as if it had cut him too.

He took in her thin, huddled figure less than three paces away from him. Alexei looked at her wan face, which not even the April sun would tan, and realized for the first time that Kathrin was beautiful, just not in the way other girls were.

He reached for Kathrin's hands and said, 'Yes, I'm homesick. Yes, I'd like to go home. But—'

He stopped. She'd already pulled her hands back and jerked her head sharply away. Without looking at him, she said brusquely, 'You've never told me about your country. I don't know anything about you.'

Alexei shrugged and his expression became blank and dull again. Quickly and tonelessly, he said, 'There's nothing to tell you. Not any more. It used to be beautiful, my home, I mean the village . . . But now—'

He went quiet. He'd never hated her – he didn't hate Germans, not all of them, just the wolves among them. He was young and since he was a child he'd been taught that in Germany, like every country in the world, there were oppressed workers who were fighting for freedom. He'd been taught that these people were admirable and united with his country by the same idea: they too were fighting for the goal that his fellow Russians had already accomplished. This was all as self-evident to him as the sun and the earth, and the houses in his village. He'd never doubted it.

Then the war came. He'd left his village and become a soldier. Later, in October 1942, he'd seen his home country again. He remembered the exact day, 27 October, when he'd stood in front of what had once been his village.

For a long time, he'd faced the grey pile of rubble that had been his parents' house and had felt no pain. He'd only felt a vast emptiness in the place where the pain had been.

He'd never found his parents or seen his sister again.

He was still so young – just twenty-four – but his hatred wasn't indiscriminately aimed at all things German. He'd fought against the fascists but he never forgot what he'd been taught in his youth. In fact, after that day in October 1942, he'd held onto his beliefs more tightly; that there were workers in Germany, and among these workers, there were comrades.

Then a bullet had grazed his head, and he'd fallen into German hands, weak and having lost a lot of blood. They'd tortured him in their prisoner-of-war camps. They'd brought him to this farm in the middle of Germany.

He'd seen this woman but he hadn't hated her. She wasn't a comrade; she knew about them but had never tried to find out about their cause. On the other hand, she wasn't one of those wolves either. He'd known this the very first day he'd caught sight of her ashen, stricken face at the window while he was waiting in the yard. And with every day that passed, he'd grown more certain that she was good and that dormant powers lay in her that, once kindled, would teach her how to love and hate.

At that moment, as he sat silently next to Kathrin, he couldn't have explained how all of this had happened – from wanting to help this helpless woman to his deep affection for her. He'd never be able to explain it.

'And what's it like now, Alexei – at home?'

She sat and listened while he told her, carefully putting one word on top of the other so that his shaky blocks of language didn't collapse; and as he did so, she moved closer towards him, never taking her eyes off his mouth, which was forming German syllables, painstakingly but clearly.

'My sister's name was Natalya,' he said. 'We called her Natasha. She could laugh! She could sing! Like no one else in the village—' He swallowed, and now the blocks of language his story was resting on began to wobble. 'I don't know what happened to her. Maybe they shot her. Maybe they kidnapped her and took her to Germany as a forced labourer.'

Kathrin laid an arm across his shoulder, a simple, heartfelt gesture that made words unnecessary. The two said nothing.

Finally, gathering herself to sound as calm as he did, and choosing her words carefully, Kathrin said: 'The farmer' (not 'my husband') – 'The farmer wrote to me. They shot all the people in a village, with machine guns.'

The Russian nodded, his eyes dark with pain and anger. It was as if she'd said: 'Your father, your mother, your brother – they were all put up against the wall and shot.'

Kathrin's hand slid off his shoulder, and she cried out

in desperation, 'Why don't you hate me? You have every reason to! Why not kill me? I'm one of them—' She started crying, her lean shoulders trembling.

'No,' said Alexei, 'no, no, you're not one of them, not you.' He hesitated, then he said it aloud after all: 'My good Katja.' He pulled her into his arms, and her tears turned to dark patches on his worn army shirt.

Alexei stroked her head carefully with his large hand. She felt the rough skin of his fingers on her face. She didn't look about. She wasn't afraid of being seen by the neighbours.

They went back to work.

The Russian steered the plough, and Kathrin led the horse up and down the furrows, up and down.

From then on, the prisoner of war and the farmer's wife sat on the upturned trough next to the pump every evening, talking or sitting together in silence. There was a lot of work to do in May, and time was racing on, but despite their exhaustion, they still found time for that one hour of the day and spent the other twenty-three hours living for it. They called what they felt for each other friendship, and sometimes they even believed that friendship was what they felt for each other.

8.

Even though Kathrin and Alexei were friendly when they greeted each other in the mornings and talked during the day, they took extreme precautions when it came to their evening encounters. They sat together for the hour that Frieda went over to see her best friend, Liesel Weckerling, and parted as soon as they heard the door clanging and voices over at the neighbour's farm that announced Frieda's return.

But one evening, Frieda stayed in. Alexei and Kathrin sat at the table and waited, but Frieda made no sign of leaving. The three of them sat there in silence as dusk stole into the corners of the room, obscuring the outlines of the furniture.

The Russian and the young woman exchanged a look. Then they stood up, went out into the yard and sat down on the trough, and Frieda stared at them from the kitchen window, a stupefied expression on her face.

She had no idea what was going on. To her, Kathrin had become a dangerous riddle. The same Kathrin who'd once scurried around the house, all small and cowed, and who'd readily and humbly followed her orders – that Kathrin had simply gone out into the yard with the blasted Russki – and not a word of explanation!

For a while, Frieda stood there seriously wondering whether she was right in the head. Slowly, she felt bile rising: why was she just sitting out there with a stranger who was no concern of hers? A decent woman ought to feel nothing but contempt for him! How often had Heinrich told her that Russians weren't proper people – those Reds just wanted to destroy everything, took farms away from farmers and killed anyone with money or a bit of property in their own country.

Kathrin, Heinrich and she were the kind of people the Reds would take everything from if, God forbid, they entered Germany. She had to tell Kathrin this. Things wouldn't end well if she wasted nice words on a man who'd slit their throats given half the chance.

When Kathrin returned to the kitchen later, Frieda, trying to soften her voice and coat it in motherly affection, said very gently, 'Listen, Kathrin, I need a word with you.'

'What's the matter?' asked Kathrin over her shoulder.

Frieda didn't let this put her off. She was sitting on the kitchen chair, her rump bulging over the narrow wooden seat, and with one foot she pulled a low stool towards her across the flagstones.

'Sit down with me awhile!'

Reluctantly, Kathrin did what she was told, although she wanted to turn in for the night. Suppressing a sigh, she sat down on the stool, her head lowered, her face hidden by the shadow of the heavy kitchen table. Only her blonde parting gleamed in the light.

Frieda had never been one to choose her words carefully. She didn't know how to gradually feel her way towards other people. Instead, she barged right into their deepest feelings. In a few words her voice lost its tinge of motherly affection. Swept up by her outrage, the coarse woman used coarse language. Gibbering angrily, she vented all her misgivings and the fury that had been brewing while she'd listened at the window. Her words refuelled her anger until she lost control of her voice and lapsed into her old thunderous scolding as if she were still the mistress of the house and Kathrin, the shy, trembling creature of the past.

As she talked, she peered intently into Kathrin's face. But Kathrin had pulled up her shoulders, and her features, pale yellow and blurred in the shadows, didn't show whether she agreed with what she was hearing.

'For Devil's sake, are you even listening to me?' Frieda said, breaking off for a moment.

The light glanced off Kathrin's blonde hair for a moment; she'd nodded almost imperceptibly.

'Well, then, tell me what you find so blooming fascinating about the lad? What would people think if they see you sitting with him in the yard? I'm surprised my eyes don't pop out of my head with shame! A German woman, even wasting a word on a Russki! Bad enough that he already sits at our table when by rights he should be in the barn . . . the—'

Finally, Kathrin lifted her head. She was biting her bottom lip, and in her eyes, which were as usually as pale as water, green sparks had appeared.

Frieda shut up.

Kathrin squeezed her hands between her knees and said quietly, 'You don't get it, Frieda. Alexei is good and helpful. You can't lock him in the barn like an animal. You spur him on like a slave driver – you'd use a whip if it was down to you. You resent every morsel of food you have to give him. Do you really not realize how cruel and unfair that is? He's a person, just like us!'

Frieda smacked the table with the flat of her hand.

'But he's not, that's exactly the point!' Her voice cracked. 'The Russians aren't real people! They're stupid, dirty, cruel and crawling with lice—' She stopped abruptly.

A smile had broken out on Kathrin's face that now turned into a cheerful, whole-hearted laugh: no, no one could make her believe these things, neither Frieda nor Heinrich – not even the whole village. Alexei was good and clever, and as clean as a man can be, so why shouldn't other Russians be like him or similar? Why would the Russian who'd come to their farm be any different from the rest? No, it was too silly an idea.

Frieda stared uncomprehendingly at Kathrin's flushed face and suddenly saw something new: her skin was no longer wan and grey but had a healthy, milky sheen. Her lips, normally pinched into a thin line, were fuller and bright red . . .

In a hushed voice, Frieda quickly asked, 'Kathrin, is there something going on between you and him?' She was appalled by her own question.

The young woman raised her arms, her hands fluttering helplessly. Her cry of 'No, no, no!' trembled with such deep horror that it convinced her sister-in-law outright. She'd never do that! She felt ashamed of her own thoughts. Kathrin was a German woman, her brother's wife – how could she suspect her like that? It was ridiculous, it was crazy, it was completely impossible!

'Sorry,' she stammered, 'I wasn't trying to – I mean, honestly—'

Kathrin had already stood up and left the kitchen.

Frieda stayed where she was, deeply dismayed. How

could she have said such a thing? If Heinrich knew. Ohgodohgodohgod ... She tugged in agitation at her thick, red fingers, struggled to her feet and wandered nervously from the wall to the table and back. Now Kathrin was mortally offended. What if she wrote to Heinrich and told him? Lord, what a row there'd be! She had to make it up to her, at all costs.

With a deep sigh, the woman dropped back down onto her chair, her big, brown eyes wide and helpless. She'd never say something like that again, no matter how much Kathrin babbled on about the Russian.

And in her frightened confusion, Frieda Marten firmly resolved never to complain about him eating at the table again and never to scold Kathrin for keeping his company in the yard. She was an odd one – always had been – but she'd never stoop so low as to carry on with a Russki!

For a long time, the woman sat there in the kitchen, her shoulders slumped, her hands restless, fretting more in one hour than she usually did in a week of her busy life.

By now, Kathrin had felt her way through the dark hall and up the stairs; but when she reached the top step, she stopped and sat down. Not to bed just yet! Not under her dull feather eiderdown! She turned around and went back down the stairs, clinging onto the banister, then crossed the yard to the barn.

Dusk was falling on the farm. The cowshed, barn and house, in which dim yellow lights blinked like eyes, looked like three black dice thrown by some giant hand. The dark flames of the poplars by the fence shot up into the night. Sleepy bird noises. Somewhere in the village, a dog yowled, another answered, and for minutes their yapping tore through the smooth silence, then was swallowed by the deep-blue expanse. Nothing but the dull lowing of the cows remained, the muffled clinking of their chains and the tired stamp of a horse's hoof.

Kathrin unlocked the barn door and signalled to Alexei.

Suddenly, an air-raid warning howled, cutting through the illusory peace of the countryside: it was the hundredth time it had sounded that year, but each time it cut right through to the core. They heard sirens coming from the nearby county town. Someone on the village road yelled 'Lights out!'

Alexei looked up at the sky and said in a strange voice, 'They come every night now.'

'They're flying to Berlin,' said Kathrin. 'Always Berlin. Those poor folk . . .'

Alexei pointed to the weak light in the kitchen window. 'The woman—?'

'She'll have lit a candle. Whenever planes fly over, she sits in the kitchen and prays.'

'And you – are you afraid?'

'I don't know.' But when she heard the distant roar of the bomber squadron, an unvarying, uncaring, terrifying sound, she ducked. The village was deathly quiet as if holding its breath. Kathrin saw that Alexei's upturned face now wore a hopeful expression. She was shocked. She too looked up at the sky, where the moon hung in a milky haze.

The drone of the bombers was coming dangerously close; they were flying very far overhead. Kathrin blurted out, 'Sometimes I wish they would bomb this place to bits . . . the whole farm. It has nothing to do with me any more . . .'

The planes were now above them. 'Come on,' said Kathrin, 'when the alarm has sounded, there's no one out on the streets.'

They walked through the gate, past two or three farmhouses, and then they were already in the fields. Their shoulders touched as they squeezed close together to walk along the narrow strip at the edge. To their right was the cow paddock, its wires stretching like silver strings from one post to the other.

A ditch separated the paddock from the adjoining clover fields, and was filled with stagnant, gleaming water. They didn't look for the plank that served as a bridge: Alexei simply jumped over and then reached his hand out to Kathrin. She leaned on him more heavily than necessary.

They sat down in the grass, which was already damp from the rising mist. The May nights were still chilly, and Kathrin pulled her knees in, shivering. Silently, the Russian hung his jacket over her shoulders.

Finally, Kathrin said, 'You have to know this, Alexei.' She turned to face him, looking very pallid in the moonlight. 'I couldn't say a word against those two. They were always right, and I had to keep my mouth shut. They didn't treat me badly – you mustn't think that, Alexei. They're rough folk, but not bad people. He's never hit me, although sometimes I wish he had. It would've been easier to accept than his contempt. He ignored me and only talked to Frieda – she was the one he discussed everything with. He went to her when he was worried, never me . . .' Kathrin stopped talking, and on her narrow face red blotches burned.

She carried on, her voice wavering. 'Just some kind of pet, that's what I was, just part of the deal, a thing they could shoo from the room. I wasn't a person to him. He's so healthy and strong and laughs so much and so hard . . . So why did he marry me in the first place, why?' She thumped her small fist on the ground, and the jacket slipped off her shoulders. 'Because I had a bit of money, because I brought my own property into the marriage, a few acres of land that he needed so he could be one of the big farmers. That's the only reason why! Ach—' Her voice broke and she fought back tears. 'And Father wanted me gone too. He never loved me. No one ever loved me, I was always in people's way, always useless—' Then she cried out, 'They pawned me off!' It was as if she'd been looking for that word for years and had found it at last. 'Pawned me off, pawned me off,' she repeated slowly. Exhausted, she fell silent.

She leaned back, now calmer and breathing more easily. The weight of the past few years fell away, as if she'd drawn a line under the past.

Alexei said nothing. He was a self-confident man, but now he suddenly felt helpless, shocked that she was putting herself entirely in his hands, without sparing herself or those who had steered and determined her life up until now.

He was frightened of the responsibility he'd taken on and for a long moment he miserably wished she hadn't come to him with this.

She gave him a searching look: dark shadows made his high cheekbones stand out even more, and for the first time she noticed two lines on his youthful face, running from his nostrils to his small, firm mouth, like incisions made with a knife. Kathrin waited for him to reply.

Alexei closed his eyes. *Poor Katja, good Katja . . .* Without opening them, he saw her in front of him, but her picture blurred into the image of her the day he arrived on the farm. There she was, slinking along the wall of the house, her steps dragging, her head hanging, back hunched, body trembling and slight, as if she were walking through cold autumn drizzle.

And next to her was that Frieda woman, her sister-in-law, a strapping woman with bulging hips, a crisp, red face and round, brown eyes – so full of life, so determined, so coarse and capable . . . Oh, he understood everything.

But why is she telling me all this? he thought bitterly. *Why me, of all people, a stranger, a prisoner of war? Does she really not realize what'll happen to her if she's seen talking to me here at night, by the edge of a field, as if I were her equal?*

I've always kept a clear head, always known how to take care of myself – I can't let my guard down now . . . I shouldn't have come with her here, shouldn't have listened to her, he thought. Yet there he sat next to her, helplessly succumbing to feelings of deep affection and tenderness.

After a while, Kathrin said, 'I often think about our life . . . What good did my land do Heinrich? He didn't make it in the end. The other farmers, with their inherited land, always looked down on him. And now they're all sitting here in safety, and he's out on the front . . . Only at home, that's where he could be the master. And to Frieda, I was just a handmaid, even though she's nothing but a slave herself. We all slog away, but what use is it to us?'

They heard the all-clear siren sound coming from the town, a dull, even tone that fell into a yowl at the end.

Kathrin said harshly, 'Can you make sense of it all? Heinrich takes care of his fields and when he's on leave, he slaves away to keep everything running smoothly – only to set off and destroy fields in another country and burn down other people's farms ... It's all so hard to understand.'

Alexei laid his broad hand on her fingers. She said quickly, 'No, you don't have to answer me. We have to get home. It's very late.'

They walked back the same way, holding hands.

The farm lay dark and still, as if people had never lived there. Alexei said, 'You have to lock me in the barn.' He said it matter-of-factly, as if he was past being offended by this ritual humiliation every evening.

Kathrin weighed the heavy key in her hand. Then she smiled and cried out, 'Pff, lock you in? I'd sooner whistle for it!' She put the key to her lips and whistled. 'There, I can still do it! We used to play a game to see who could whistle the loudest with a key.' She laughed.

Alexei looked at her in astonishment.

She suddenly stood on tiptoe, pulled his head towards hers and kissed him quickly and shyly. Then she ran into the house.

9.

Kathrin forgot Heinrich Marten as if he'd never existed.

Frieda got used to the Russian being around, at first grudgingly, then with resignation. That's how it was, and she couldn't change it. She didn't spy on her sister-in-law; if she was still suspicious at all, she didn't show it. And there was nothing to spy on that could have fed her suspicions. The pair of them, Alexei and Kathrin, only seldom exchanged a few words when she was around. They were calm and polite, and no stolen glances or familiar gestures passed between them.

Only once did Frieda express her astonishment about the Russian's language skills. Hadn't the farmers' overseer told her he barely spoke three words of German? But Kathrin quickly soothed her sister-in-law, saying that Alexei had been on the farm for over three months now, and must be a fast learner, having picked up many words from the two women in that time.

So, Frieda came to accept Alexei Luniev's company. To tell the truth, she began to feel something like affection towards him. He was always calm and polite, courteous but not in an obvious way, and most of all, hard-working. None of this was lost on the gruff woman, although she would never have admitted it.

When he was in the kitchen, she spoke more quietly despite herself. Had he not been Russian, she would have been able to treat him as an equal, with respect.

And so, the lives of the three went on calmly and peacefully, or so it seemed; but below that smooth surface, unbeknown to any of them, things were beginning to brew. Their repressed passion was too strong, and the barriers of obedience, duty and fear that divided one from the other were too weak.

June was hot. Pale-red dog roses were in bloom on the railway embankment, and the scent of lilac and jasmine drifted through the gardens. The mild evenings were filled with the sound of chirping crickets.

Kathrin and Alexei were sitting together on the trough by the pump.

The clear night absorbed their strained conversation, and soon they stopped talking to listen to the moving silence, their heads lowered. In the village, a harmonica was playing.

The young people in the village lived for this hour of the day. The war was far away; no artillery thunder or cries from the wounded broke the peace around the farmhouses. They kissed each other at the edges of fields and under lilac bushes.

Sometimes, the pair sitting on the trough heard the twin footsteps of a couple approaching; two shadows slid past the fence, and they watched until the sweethearts were swallowed up by the darkness again.

Then their eyes met, a spark passing from one to the other, their hands found each other and let go again, faltering between hope and hopelessness.

One evening, the village broke into their solitude.

The western sky was still red. All at once, Kathrin's name was called out from the fence. She jumped up, startled, then strolled over to the fence, trying to look casual, to greet Anders, an old farmer from the neighbourhood.

He was poking about in the sand with his stick, his eyes darting over to the Russian in the yard. 'Just thought I'd come by,' he said. 'Said to myself, why don't you go and wish Kathrin a pleasant evening . . . You're a rare sight these days.'

Kathrin shrugged. 'Why should I run about the village? There's work to do, as you know yourself.'

The old man blinked and said simply, 'You've got an able lad helping out now, so I've heard.' Kathrin said nothing. He stood there for a while longer, arms propped on the fence, letting his eyes wander about the place. At last, he left. Grinning over his shoulder, he called out, 'Say hello to his lordship, the soldier.' Kathrin walked hesitantly back over to Alexei.

'A spy', he said.

'What are you talking about? He's always been friendly towards me. When I was little, he used to give me liquorice.'

'The old man has sharp eyes,' said Alexei. His voice sounded cold and strange now. 'Be careful, German woman. Not speak any more.'

Kathrin cried in dismay, 'You don't think I'd ever betray you!'

Alexei stared at the ground.

'You know nothing. The Germans . . . I know them. I know their camps. How they tortured us, those bastards . . .'

Kathrin flushed hot with delayed fear, and her heart pounded.

They had been warned.

They forgot the warning.

*

Kathrin was coming out of the chicken coop, both hands gathering up her apron in which she was carrying eggs. She blinked into the sun. At that moment, Alexei pushed open the gate.

Kathrin stayed where she was until he pulled the cart, piled high with hay, into the yard. The young woman came nearer. The Russian nodded towards her and reached up to the seat where a bunch of dog roses lay.

No one had ever given her flowers. Heinrich Marten wasn't the type to bring his wife flowers on wedding anniversaries or birthdays. When she'd gone dancing in the inn, which was rare enough, Kathrin hadn't pinned flowers to her dress either. There was a saying: 'A girl with flowers at her breast can be kissed without request.' This was reason alone for her not to pin flowers to her dress at the dance. What would the village boys say? She'd rarely been asked to dance in the first place, but when a young man did request her hand, it was usually at the suggestion of the boy's father, who knew about old Law's dowry for his daughter.

Alexei held out the bouquet with the awkwardness of a young lad.

Kathrin, who had to hold on to the edges of her apron, shrugged.

'Oh, Alexei, that's sweet of you – but I can't take them. The eggs . . .'

He laughed and lay the flowers in her apron.

'Thank you so much, Alexei,' Kathrin said.

He looked at her. She wasn't wearing a headscarf, and her blonde hair was shimmering in the sun. He took one of the pale red roses and held it to her temple as if checking. She understood and lowered her head for him. Clumsily, he stuck it in her hair while she kept still, blushing.

He took a step back, looked at her and said, 'Beautiful, Kathrin. You are beautiful.'

'Oh, you're silly, Alexei.' Kathrin pouted but then had to laugh. He joined in.

They'd not heard the gate opening. Trude Meinhardt appeared in front of them. Kathrin went quiet and blushed even more furiously in her confusion. Alexei gave the stranger a hostile stare, but Trude Meinhardt remained neutral.

'You look pretty, Kathrin,' she said with a smile. Her stern face seemed to soften and relax. She shook her head. 'Like children . . .'

Alexei shrugged. Trude turned to look at him. His features relaxed, and the hostility in his eyes disappeared: it was good to meet a decent person. He greeted her briefly but respectfully, then spun around and left.

Kathrin followed Trude into the house. In the entrance hall, Trude plucked the rose from her hair and placed it inside her apron along with the others. Kathrin was horrified.

'There's nothing wrong with it, is there?' she asked miserably.

Trude smoothed down her tousled hair.

'No, Kathrin, of course there's nothing wrong with it. I wore flowers too when I was young. But—' she added harshly, 'you two aren't sixteen. You're not the girl and boy next door . . . Frieda doesn't need to see that.'

'Let her see it! It doesn't mean anything!'

Unruffled, Trude answered, 'Frieda wouldn't understand. She's never had a sweetheart. No man has ever given her flowers.' Before Kathrin could answer, she led the way into the kitchen.

Half an hour later, Kathrin accompanied her to the door. Trude saw that Kathrin was troubled by a question but she didn't encourage her to ask it: Kathrin needed to find the nerve herself.

They had already said their goodbyes when Kathrin said, 'You said Frieda's never had a sweetheart. Why is that? She must have been very pretty when she was younger.'

'She certainly could have had one,' Trude replied, 'but she was too fond of Heinrich and didn't want to leave him as long as there was no woman on the farm. Well, by the time he married you, it was too late for Frieda. She was in her early thirties and the men her age were already long since married. And if she was to find a younger husband – well, she'd have needed to bring something of her own into the marriage.'

'I didn't know that,' Kathrin said slowly. 'That's why she's so attached to Heinrich . . .'

After a while, she added, 'I'm often angry with her. But actually, I should feel sorry for her.'

The other woman nodded. 'She's grown bitter, you have to understand that, Kathrin,' hesitantly adding, 'and she's jealous of young couples. She can't bear to have two people who are fond of each other around her.' She left.

Kathrin stood there, motionless and sunk in thought. It took a few moments before she understood. She ran after Trude Meinhardt, out of her mind with fear; she ran down the road, drawing level with her at the inn, where she cried out, 'Trude! Trude!' Trude looked at the breathless woman without surprise. Kathrin was next to her, grabbing her hand and shouting, 'What are you trying to say? What do you mean? Do you really think that Alexei and I—'

Trude placed her hand over Kathrin's mouth. 'Don't shout, Kathrin,' she said quietly and quickly. 'Come with me. I want to show you something.'

Kathrin followed. Silently, they walked down the road, dust swirling beneath their feet as the heat beat down on the farmhouses.

The sickroom was cool and dark, the shutters were closed, and the sunlight cast broad, golden streaks through the slats. The two women sat down on the pallet, taking deep breaths in the coolness.

Without preamble, Trude said, 'I've seen nothing and I know nothing, Kathrin. And if I had – child, do you think I would talk about it?'

Kathrin lifted both hands in defence. 'It's nothing bad, I swear. It's not the way you might think. We're friends, you see. We talk and sit together in the evenings, but there's nothing else to it, I swear.' But she avoided those piercing, dark eyes, sensing that she was lying to herself and Trude, even though she was telling the truth: nothing had happened that would horrify others.

Trude talked down to her folded hands. 'But still, Kathrin, you have to be careful. In this country, among these people, even friendship is dangerous. He's a Russian, after all, and people hate Russians here. They don't see them as human and call them an inferior race. Don't look at me like that – I don't think that way, you know that. It's like there's a toxic gas in their heads, so that they can't see clearly any more and believe the craziest nonsense.' She got to her feet. Standing in front of Kathrin, she was very tall, and her face very stern and thin. 'Do you know the punishment for a German woman who has a relationship with a Russian?'

Kathrin shook her head apprehensively.

Trude crossed to the medicine cabinet, fetched a newspaper that was folded into three and threw it to Kathrin with a disgusted, angry gesture.

'There, read that!'

Kathrin unfolded the newspaper, her hands shaking. There was a picture: on a podium stood three women with shaven heads that looked strangely unreal against the grey background, round, bald and as gruesome as skulls. Glaring white signs hung around their necks. The quality of the photo was poor and the writing on the signs was blurred and illegible.

'What does it say?' Kathrin asked.

'It says "I have betrayed my Fatherland".'

Kathrin sank into a bloody fog in which the three pale, bald skulls danced. 'I have betrayed my Fatherland.' Nausea choked her, and she felt the urge to jump up and flee – anywhere, just out of this room, away from this village, this life.

Trude's face was twisted in anger and disgust as she said, 'It also says, "Spit at me! I am a Russian whore!"'

'Oh God, oh my God,' groaned Kathrin. She buried her face in her hands.

The stern voice above her said, 'People spit at them. People throw stones and dirt at them. They don't deserve any better. They're whores, after all – Russian whores, and that makes them ten times worse.'

Kathrin stood up, her face ashen, her eyes dead-looking. She felt an iciness rising from her fingertips up her arms to her heart. Trude grasped Kathrin's shoulders because it looked as if she might keel forward at any moment. Kathrin shuddered at her touch and tried to pull herself away. 'Why did you tell me all this?' she whispered.

Trude looked at her sadly. 'Oh, Kathrin, you probably hate me now. You think I despise these women because they fell in love with Russians. Yes, I wanted to give you a shake. I wanted to show you the terrible things people do in blind hatred and show you what you're up against if someone pins something on you, or finds out about your relationship with Alexei. Yes, even if it is just a friendship – who's going to believe that?' She added fiercely, 'I don't want to stand on the market square one day, watching them shave off your hair, blaming myself for not warning you.'

Kathrin walked away as if she couldn't see, dragging her feet through the dust on the road. Her head was empty; she only saw the women's shaven heads and those terrible words on the white sign: 'Russian whore'.

When she opened the kitchen door, her gaze fell on the bouquet of pale-red dog roses standing in a water glass in the middle of the table. She pulled the door closed behind her, leaned against the wall and sobbed uncontrollably.

Alexei was unloading hay. He'd seen Kathrin arrive, pallid, her shoulders sagging. He was alarmed. He jumped down from the cart, knowing it wasn't wise to go to her now – Frieda could see him from the barn. But his concern for Kathrin drove him on.

He ran into the house and opened the kitchen door.

Kathrin was leaning on the wall, racked with sobs. She didn't try to fend off Alexei when he embraced her and pulled her head to his chest.

He didn't need to ask; in a tired, flat voice, she told him what she'd seen and heard. He took a step back. She said, 'My God, how can people be so cruel? Why do they stomp all over such beautiful feelings? You can't sentence a person to death for loving someone.'

Alexei had turned away and was standing by the table. He took a rose out of the glass and started pulling off its petals with such cold rigour that Kathrin cried out: 'Leave the poor flowers alone, Alexei!'

He spun around, his lips pressed into a single, thin line. 'I knew it,' he said, 'I should have told you. Now I have to leave before it's too late.'

No! Kathrin wanted to scream, but she couldn't. In a barely audible tone, she asked, 'But how are you going to leave? Will you run away?'

He laughed. 'Run away? Without papers, without clothes? No, there's an easier way. You go to the man who brought me here and tell him I do bad work. Tell him too, if you want, that I go after you. Then they will send me back to the camp. Your worries are gone.'

'What will happen to you, Alexei?' Kathrin struggled to ask.

He waved his hand dismissively. *Don't think about that.* He looked at her face, saw her doubts and how she was wavering between firmness and cowardice. He felt like screaming the things they would do to him into her face. Dragged to a factory as a forced labourer, or perhaps to a concentration camp, from which there was only one way out – a mass grave.

All his thoughts and feelings were now tied to this woman: he was bitterly disappointed to discover a flicker of relief in her eyes at his suggestion. But still, he understood. She'd never seen death at close quarters, and this must make her own death inconceivable.

He went to the door; he was still waiting. He pushed down the handle, already having lost hope. He turned around one more time. She hurled herself at his chest, putting both arms around him, crying in desperation, 'Don't go, Alexei, don't go!'

He stroked her hair. 'Katyusha, it's better this way. Think of yourself. . .' But he sounded unconvincing, and he knew it.

'It's all going to be all right,' Kathrin said. 'I'm not afraid of what will come. You mustn't go.'

She didn't believe that everything would be all right. Today she'd seen her fate. But weeks, perhaps months, lay between today and the time when all of this would come to an end.

'I would die if you went away,' she said. She put her arm around his neck. 'I love you.'

He bent down and kissed her mouth and hands.

10.

Around this time, people in the village started whispering about tawdry goings-on at Martens' farm: Kathrin Marten was on more intimate terms with her prisoner of war than a soldier's wife ought to be. People said they'd noticed this and noticed that, but no one knew anything specific, and they took care never to say anything directly. A suspicion alone could have terrible consequences if said aloud. No one really knew exactly how the rumour had started – perhaps old Anders had been chinwagging or else it was due to Kathrin Marten's transformation, which the women noticed.

No wonder; after all, everyone in the village knew everyone else – they'd all grown up together. Everyone knew the fortunes and problems, births and deaths, quarrels and agreements that went on in every farm. Gossip flourished: Liesel Weckerling had a new admirer; Grete Anders was wearing a muslin dress to the dance that cost much more than she could afford; the Fritz's cow with the blaze on its face had had trouble calving; the landlord at the village inn beat his wife when he was drunk; Farmer Wernitz sent a large parcel from France every month; Trude Meinhardt's boy did the best in tests. They knew each other inside out, and the women in their kitchens and the men at the inn ranted and spouted, analysed and were scandalized by every little titbit, from

Grete Anders' muslin dress to Farmer Wernitz's latest parcel from France.

When Kathrin Marten walked down the road to the baker's, she was followed by furtive looks. She's got a skip in her step today! She's got her chin up! What a bright blouse she's wearing! Some women stopped her and tried to draw her into conversation, not bothering to hide their insinuations: How was the prisoner getting along? Was she satisfied?

Kathrin, who had wised up by now, ignored these sometimes heavy-handed, sometimes subtle hints. Her answers were measured and polite: yes, she was satisfied, yes, he was a good worker, and a good, diligent man all round. She cleverly changed the subject to the harvest, their children and their husbands on the front. Then she said goodbye and left the women behind, their curiosity unsatisfied. They returned to their houses none the wiser, gloating over the mysterious rumours but not actually knowing a thing.

However, there was one girl in the village with a sharp tongue and even sharper eyes. She picked up on some things that others failed to see. Liesel Weckerling wore her bright blonde plaits in swirls around her head; she was pretty and cheeky, and people said that she changed lovers as often as she changed her shirts. Her latest beau was a worker from the county town, a serious-looking, dark-haired man who was blind in one eye and so couldn't serve in the army. Head over heels she was, and no one could understand why, because he wasn't a looker, couldn't dance and was quite ungainly.

That girl's ears pricked up when talk turned to the Marten woman and her prisoner. She listened with an alertness that went far beyond her usual nosiness. There was a special reason for this. Some two years back, Liesel had had a little romance with Heinrich Marten. She'd taken a shine to him, that handsome, well-built man, and had flirted with him. A few times, he'd even walked her home from the inn and kissed her at the front door.

Perhaps Heinrich had bragged to a friend. Perhaps the pair had been seen in front of her door and someone had tipped Kathrin off. Whatever the case, the Marten woman had found out about the kissing. The next day, she ran into Liesel. Without saying a word, she'd just looked at the girl, and Liesel thought she could see contempt in her eyes. It was a look she'd never forgotten.

Liesel couldn't stand the quiet, reclusive Marten woman in the first place because her own parents were always holding Kathrin up as a role model for their flighty daughter. Now, jealousy was stirred into the mix; subconsciously, Liesel felt a flicker of envy towards the woman who was married to brawny, good-looking Heinrich. This added to her aversion to the Marten woman, a feeling she'd not managed to get over in the two years since her dalliance with Heinrich. Liesel would pin anything she could on Kathrin Goody-Two-Shoes, Little Miss Shy-and-Alluring. Oh, to throw her a glance full of contempt, to look down on her even once, that's all she wanted! And so Liesel kept her ears pricked for any scraps of news that might feed the rumour about her and the prisoner. Her darting eyes were always open, and she was the first witness to something that hardened the rumours into certainty.

One day she arrived to meet her sweetheart, the serious, dark-haired, half-blind man, in a state of excitement with flushed cheeks. Beaming with satisfaction, she told him that she'd surprised Kathrin Marten – he knew the one, the thin, blonde woman from the neighbouring farm – with her young fella, the Russian. 'A Russian, fancy that, Paul!' They'd been up on the fields turning hay, and Liesel had seen them kissing. 'Brazenly kissing, as if they were all alone in the world! I saw it with my own eyes!'

Paul let the girl's arm go and said drily, 'I see. And what else?'

Liesel looked baffled. 'What else? Isn't that enough? Kissing, I tell you – a Russian! Oh, that one, always pretending to be so chaste, so lah-di-dah ... and then a Russian!' Her mousy grey eyes glittered with pleasure.

Paul looked at her. Not one jot of the laughing, triumphant girl's Schadenfreude was reflected in his dark eyes. 'And what else?' he asked one more time.

'God, you can ask such daft questions,' she cried. 'Silly-billy! I have to tell Heinrich – oh, what a face he'll make! She'll be out on her ear, that loose—' She fell silent, seeing his anger. He was so unlike the other men she'd known, which was also why she liked him the most.

They'd walked out of the village by now and were already in the fields, alone under the starry sky.

'You're not going to tell anyone about this,' he said, 'not Heinrich or anyone else.'

'Oh, but I shall – now of all times!' she said. But her voice shook with dread, and she felt suddenly afraid of the man's lifelessly staring eye. The remote, silent field scared her too, and the thought flitted through her head that he could hit her and no one would hear her scream.

Paul grabbed the girl's arm, coming up very close to her face and growling with anger. 'You'll say nothing, Liesel, you hear, nothing! Otherwise . . .' He faltered as it hurt him to say it, but in the end, he did: 'Otherwise, that'll be the last you see of me. It'll be over between us, for once and for all.'

The girl was appalled. No, anything but that! That was too high a price . . .

She spoke quickly and tried to sound scornful as if she was over the whole thing. 'God, Paul, what a fuss you can kick up! Frightening me like this when it's got nothing to do with you. You don't even know the Marten woman. But if you insist . . . OK, I'll not say anything. The others will notice soon enough.'

He was still gripping her arm. 'Promise me,' he said, 'cross your heart.' Liesl still didn't understand. Airily, she said, 'OK, cross my heart . . .' She saw him breathe out.

He sat down in the grass and pulled her down towards him. Then he tried to reason with her. 'You have to understand, Liesel – if this gets out, it could cost them their necks. No, it's got nothing to do with me. But in the end, it does! They're people like you or me and they love each other like we do, and you can't condemn them for that. The man's Russian but, my God, he can't help that. You can't help being German. Being born in a different country doesn't make him worse than us.'

'But even the overseer said that Russians aren't real people.'

'Don't let anyone tell you that. "Not real people" . . . There are good and bad folk everywhere.' He clasped her hands and shook his head: in those silly little hands lay the lives of two people.

Liesel leaned her head lazily against his chest. What an oddball her Paul was . . . He spoke into her hair. 'My final word, listen. If you don't hold your tongue, it's over between us, get it?'

The man in the dun-grey uniform trudged, sweating, down the country road, which seemed to be bubbling in the heat of the white-hot sun. Sticky black puddles glistened on the melted asphalt. The soldier's boots churned up grey fountains of dust on the narrow footpath under the cherry trees.

He stopped, wiped the sweat off his forehead with the back of his hand and looked intently at the fields on either side: the crops looked good, their stalks high and bending under heavy ears of corn, plentiful with grain.

He grabbed a handful of wheat and rubbed it between his fingers. The grains sprang open, dry and golden. He nodded in satisfaction. It would be a good, rich harvest. He longed to be here when they reaped the crops, walking through the fields, scythe in hand, listening to the swishing of the falling stalks, loading and bringing in the hay. Ach, this damned war!

In a few days, he'd be back in the trenches, charging at the enemy, burrowing into the crumbling earth like a mole, crouching under the high-pitched whistle of bullets, sweating, filthy, the rat-tat-tat of machine guns, the roar of heavy tanks and the cries of the wounded in his ears. This bloody war!

He placed his cap back on his head. Three or four days of rest, thank God. He'd check on the farm, eat his fill, sleep his fill, his wife next to him in bed – that all made it bearable . . . He sighed, ready to walk on, the village pulling him towards it like a magnet, its pointed church tower sticking up as thin as a needle against the woods in the shimmering heat of the sky.

He heard the horse-drawn cart juddering up behind him, turned and recognized old Anders in the coachman's seat. He waved to him. Anders tipped his cap with the handle of his whip, pulled tight on the reins and cried, 'Hey, Heinrich, climb up!' The soldier swung himself aloft, and the horses walked on, hooves thudding dully on the grey, softened asphalt.

'How's tricks?' The soldier pulled out a pack of Russian Papirosa with their distinctive long cardboard mouthpiece and offered one to the farmer. Anders looked sceptically at the foreign cigarette, sniffed it and then stuck it behind his ear. Then he replied. 'Tricks? How are they ever? Lots of work, lots of trouble – same as always . . .'

Heinrich gave Anders a sidelong glance and saw that he'd grown old, awfully old. His short hair had turned silvery grey, and his face, marked by countless lines, was pinched beneath his cheekbones. Just four months earlier, when he'd last seen him, the farmer's face had been smooth and spry.

The younger man shrugged. 'Well, there's always lots to do. And trouble? There'll be a hell of a harvest this year—'

The old man dismissed his words with a tired wave of his hand. Momentarily, he leaned towards Heinrich and said confidentially, 'Well, you know what I'm talking about. Grete, that strumpet—'

'No, I don't know,' said Heinrich and only then did he realize that four months is a long time in which many things can happen.

Anders let out a whistle and jerked hard on the reins. 'Go on!' Heinrich stared uneasily at the old man's withered hands and wished he'd run into Liesel Weckerling with her wheat-blonde plaits instead. It'd have been a nicer welcome than this grumpy old man.

In an alarmingly jaunty tone, Anders continued: 'A nice life my Grete leads. That strumpet goes off to town and knocks around with those young SS blowhards!'

'No, no, no, don't you go badmouthing the SS! They've got guts, those lads, they're always first in line on the front.'

'And when it comes to the girls too,' said the old man scathingly. 'Especially with the girls, oh, they've got guts. And now my own granddaughter! Swans into the village, flaunting herself, puffed up like a peacock in her new finery. Had on a see-through little number the other day. "Muslin," she tells me, as pink as candyfloss. So, Heinrich, you tell me, how can she afford such a thing? I'll tell you how! By jumping into bed with one fella after the other – those pigs!' Anders spat out the last word. 'But when she comes running to me with a little brat on the way, I'll throw her out, just you wait!' He nodded, and his loose jowls shook.

He's got awfully old, Heinrich thought, and slid agitatedly back and forth in his seat. He wasn't even supposed to overhear this kind of talk: it counted as incitement, hostile to the German people. Although when he pictured Grete, that little snub-nose, pretty brunette and such a bright girl, he thought it couldn't be easy for her grandfather to think of her out on the streets.

'You just don't understand, Anders,' he said. 'Throw her out? Come on! It's an honour for a German woman to become a mother. And the SS are the elite. You obviously haven't heard that lots of girls these days are giving birth out of wedlock and offering their babies to the Führer, and proud of it too.'

'Proud! And unwed, hmm?' Anders glared hostilely at the healthy, tanned face of the man next to him. 'So that's the kind you've turned into? Nice views you lot have these days. In my day, little scamps like them were driven out of the home in shame and disgrace! And these days, it's all honour and pride and giving birth for the Führer!' He gave a nasty laugh, showing his disgust. Suddenly his gaze fell on Heinrich's uniform jacket, which bore a black cross with a silver edge.

'Ah, a decorated man, are you now? Well, congratulations! Is that why you're on leave?'

Heinrich's ears pricked up in suspicion. What on earth had got into the old man? His congratulations didn't sound genuine at all. But that only made him stick out his chest and gloat even more. 'The Iron Cross. You do what you can. And the Führer shows his appreciation.'

'Fan of the war, are you?' grunted the old man morosely.

Heinrich's happiness to be home and his unease when he'd imagined himself back in the trenches in a few days suddenly vanished. He said quickly and very loudly, 'We know in the end what we're fighting for. You wait till we've captured Ukraine – my, God, you should see the fields! They stretch to the horizon, as far as the eye can see, nothing but wheat, the like of which you've never set eyes on! Stalks as tall as a man. And the soil is black and slick – that's the place to have a farm.'

Anders said nothing, and Heinrich was annoyed by his uninterested expression. If he'd seen that soil, those fields of wheat, his eyes would fall out of his head, that stubborn old mule. But that's how these folk were: they'd never left the village, were stuck in their ways and never got enthusiastic about anything.

They'd turned the corner at the woods, and the village lay before them as if placed on a giant outstretched hand. Heinrich sniffed the air. 'I can already smell the lake,' he said, his bad mood quickly vanishing. The lake! The farms! The church! There – Trude Meinhardt's house, her front garden, overgrown with marigolds and blue delphiniums.

The large, loud man sat as still as a child in front of a wonderful present, and as happy as a kid, he jumped down from the coach. 'I'm turning off here. Anders, see you around!'

'Say hello to Kathrin for me!' the old man called after him. 'Boy, is *she* going to be happy—'

Heinrich stood there, not saying a word, seized by a feeling of unease. There was a tone of scorn in the old man's frail voice that the soldier didn't understand.

He marched off quickly and soon reached his farm; while he was standing beneath the arch of the gate, his wife came out of the house and, without seeing him, made off for the stable.

'Kathrin!' he cried.

She stopped in her tracks, her back to him and stood there momentarily as if turned to stone. Slowly she turned to face him. Her eyes looked as if they'd been extinguished. He walked over to her.

'You?' Kathrin asked, as if she were trying to remember who he was.

Heinrich laughed. 'Ha, didn't expect me, did you? Nice surprise, huh?' He suddenly stopped talking, feeling awkward; she nodded mechanically, her smile lopsided. He tried to take her in his arms, but she took a step back.

'Don't,' she begged, sounding choked.

'What's the matter, what's the matter?' he boomed. 'Surely a man's allowed to kiss his own wife?' He threw his arms around her and kissed her.

Her lips remained firmly closed. When he let her go, suddenly deflated, she threw a timid look over her shoulder. 'If someone sees us here—'

Heinrich forced himself to lighten up. 'Come now, still such a coy young lamb? Then let's go in, I'm as hungry as a wolf,' adding, close to her ear, 'hungry for you . . .'

'Frieda's in the kitchen, you go on ahead and get yourself something to eat,' Kathrin cried. 'I quickly have to feed the hens.' And she rushed off, so fast that her light skirt flapped against her tanned calves.

Heinrich stared after her, unsettled, uncomprehending, now noticing for the first time that she was bareheaded, and that her hair was washed and falling in soft waves almost down to her shoulders. Four months is a long time. He didn't remember his wife being so blonde; for a moment, he imagined that she'd coloured her hair. And the way she ran! Like a girl . . . She seemed to have filled out a little too, no longer the angular little waif she used to be.

Heinrich shook his head. What a fuss she always made! Well, her coyness, that'd pass. Must've been the shock of seeing him standing at the door, unannounced.

Smiling to himself, he went into the house.

Kathrin found Alexei in the cool twilit barn. Sunlight, swirling with billions of dust motes, was flooding through the big doors.

She threw herself onto his chest and put her arms around him, pressing her head against his bare shoulder.

Alexei stroked her back. 'Katyusha, sweetheart, what is it?' He felt her trembling.

'He's back,' she whispered.

The man froze. Finally, he would come face to face with the stranger, this hated man, and stare him in the eye, scrutinizing him. *Who are you? Someone who carries out orders to murder women and children? Who are you that you were allowed to marry Kathrin?*

'Help me, Alexei,' Kathrin begged. 'What should I do? I'll run away. I can't face him like this—'

'Do you feel guilty?' he asked.

She shook her head. 'No, Alexei, I don't belong to him any more, you know that.'

'But he is your husband – you're still married,' Alexei cried in a pained tone.

They said nothing more. They were both thinking the same thing.

In a fit of jealousy, Alexei shook Kathrin and said, 'You will sleep with him—'

'No,' she cried, 'no, Alexei, never! I'll fend him off, I'd rather he killed me . . .'

'You can't, he'll beat you!' Alexei cried, exasperated. She

had never seen him like this; his eyes were ablaze, and he was trying to control himself, but the dreadful image of Kathrin in the arms of another man almost drove him mad.

He knew he was being unfair and was ashamed of it, but he had to make her suffer. Pushing her away, he cried, 'And you avoid me! You refuse me! You're still fond of him. Leave!' He turned away from her abruptly, and his bare back shimmered in the gloom.

Kathrin stood there, devastated. At any moment, Heinrich could have come in and found them there. She felt a sweat break out on her forehead. She wasn't angry or sad, but her mind had gone blank, as if she were swimming in a grey fog.

'Don't torture me, Alexei,' she said. He turned around, half-defeated, to face her again. Her hands were raised, pleading. In just two steps, he was at her side and clasped them.

'Katyusha, forgive me!'

She leaned against him with her eyes closed and felt his warm, smooth skin on her neck and arms. 'I won't let him touch me,' she said. She stroked his hair; it had grown back in the last few months and was sun-bleached and turning curly. He kissed her.

When Kathrin came into the kitchen, her husband was sitting at the table, a mountain of sandwiches in front of him, and Frieda was leaning against the hob, beaming and wearing a crisply starched apron, as if she had something to celebrate.

Heinrich had taken off his jacket and rolled up his shirt sleeves, already very much at home. His black hair was combed and plastered to his head with water, as glossy as paint.

'He's been given the Iron Cross!' Frieda shouted triumphantly. Her cheeks were like polished apples, red and round, and her brown eyes shone with so much pride and sisterly love that Kathrin had no choice; she bent down to admire the black medal on the uniform hanging over Heinrich's chair. As she straightened up again, she whispered close to Heinrich's ear: 'How many people did you kill for that?'

He jerked away as if she'd slapped him, putting the half-eaten sandwich back on his plate. 'Would you like a cup of coffee?' Kathrin asked. 'Or rather a beer?'

'Beer,' he mumbled, stunned, his face dark red. He thought he'd misheard her. The hulking man couldn't grasp this abrupt change in his wife's behaviour.

His baffled gaze followed her as she fetched a beer from the pantry and a hint of lust sprang into his eyes. How gracefully she moved! How supple her back was, and how softly her fair hair flowed over her neck!

Heinrich Marten hadn't exactly lived like a monk while he was away. He'd ogled many a woman and slept with a few, some blonde, some brunette, some passive, some lustful – God, what was a man supposed to do – sweat it all out through his ribs? And the women in Russia weren't half bad – pert breasts, comely hips. They'd set up brothels for German soldiers in the towns. A private tried to persuade him that the girls there were forced into it, innocents, dragged in from the countryside or some village. But Heinrich didn't believe him. He hadn't come across a virgin yet. They were all jaded and no longer any fun.

He'd never actually thought about Kathrin during it all. Sometimes he'd felt a hint of guilt but always found an excuse, the most important one being that he might be dead tomorrow. Why not enjoy life? Schnapps and chicks were just a part of it. Here today, gone tomorrow.

When Kathrin set the beer down in front of him, he tried to pull her onto his lap. She twisted herself out of his embrace with a soft movement so as not to offend him. He pawed her coarsely. 'Little lamb, you coy thing . . .' Then with a wide leer, he said, 'Well, you've scrubbed up! And very nice too! Didn't know I had such a pretty wife . . .'

Her cheeks flushed briefly, and she struggled to find an answer, but he'd already turned to Frieda and was asking, 'How's the farm running? Everything as it should be?'

Soon the siblings were deep in conversation about the farm, the harvest and livestock, leaving Kathrin out as usual. She went to leave the kitchen, but her husband said, 'And how are you getting on with the Russki?'

Frieda tilted her head from side to side: oh, very well, he knew how to work on a farm.

Kathrin listened, her body tense. No, there was not a word about how he ate with them in the house, no mention of any intimacy between him and Kathrin. She suddenly realized that she had nothing to fear. The pair of them were just chatting about the farmhand Alexei whose feelings meant as little to them as the farm dog's. She was both offended and relieved.

Later, they did the rounds through the barn and stables. Kathrin tagged along, thinking that Heinrich might run into the prisoner and that she might need to be there if so. She didn't know what would happen when the two men met but she had a vague sense of unease that it might be terrible. Heinrich would surely realize in an instant how much Alexei hated him and how much he loved his wife when he saw him face to face.

They went into the cowshed. Inside, the air was sweltering and sticky. Black flies covered everything – the hayrack, the troughs, and the rumps of the listless cows that were swishing their tails at their tormentors.

The Russian was walking down the gangway with two pails of water. His bare torso was slick with sweat, his white-blond hair curling around his dark-brown face, making his sharp cheekbones stand out more prominently than ever. He stood to one side to let the three pass.

Heinrich stopped. He sized up the young man from head to toe and asked, 'What's your name?'

The other shrugged, naked hostility in his eyes. Kathrin squeezed in next to her husband. Alexei lowered his eyes and said quickly, 'Alexei Ivanovich Luniev.'

'Do you speak German?'

The Russian's lively face became dull, indifferent. 'Nothing German. I understand leetle German, very leetle—'

Kathrin smiled.

'And what's your profession?'

Alexei didn't understand, Alexei hadn't understood a single word. He murmured, 'I – not understand.' Now he seemed almost gaga.

Kathrin had a childish urge to join in the game. She translated for him. 'What do you do in Russia? Understand? *Rabota?*'

'Ah—' Now it seemed to dawn on him. He made a sweeping gesture around the stable with his hand, as if he was referring to the whole farm. 'Cow, horse, yes?' He made ploughing and digging motions.

'A farmer, then?' Heinrich asked, and Alexei nodded. He picked up the pails of water and pushed past the three of them to avoid any more questions. Heinrich watched him go, tapped his finger on his forehead and, without lowering his voice, said, 'A bit dim, that fella, right?'

'He doesn't understand much German,' said Frieda. 'Just what he's picked up from us.'

Heinrich carried on, stopping at the pregnant mare's stall to rub between her ears.

'Make sure you call the vet in time! You women won't manage the birth by yourselves.'

Only now did Kathrin realize that the moment had passed. None of the terrible scenes she'd feared had taken place. Neither man had lunged at the other's throat; instead, they had remained calm and even-tempered, the only way things could be between master and servant.

She was ashamed of the game she'd played in front of the brother and sister.

'Blasted heat in here,' Heinrich growled. He pulled his shirt over his head, and his white torso stood out in the dim light, his chest separated from his ruddy neck by a sharp line.

The Russian was grooming the bull calf, whose black-and-white flecked coat shimmered like dull silk. Heinrich watched him attentively, then nodded with satisfaction. It wasn't clear whether his attention was focused on the man or the bull.

Out of nowhere, he announced loudly and blithely, 'He's a good size, that young 'un.' He was pointing his thumb at the man but using the same gesture and tone as if he were assessing an animal.

He went into the stall and strode over to the Russian. Without realizing it, he assumed a vain pose that invited comparison with the Russian's physique.

Both were roughly the same height. Nevertheless, the Russian looked almost dainty next to the fleshy German.

Kathrin's laugh wiped Heinrich's look of complacency from his face, leaving it naked and empty-looking. Even the gloss of his black hair seemed to dull in his confusion. He stepped back out of the stall and, without looking at the other man or the women, left the stable.

Liesel Weckerling happened to be strolling by the fence at that moment, a hay rake slung over her shoulder. She saw Heinrich stomping across the yard and waved. He waved back, laughing.

Heinrich didn't mention the prisoner again. He snapped orders at the women, and they had to jump to attention and fulfil the never-ending wishes of the soldier on leave. Kathrin made his bed in their room and seemed almost cheerful as she hummed a song under her breath. Things had been going well so far, and she wasn't afraid of what would happen that night: she'd pretend to be ill or complain of pains, then he'd leave her in peace. But when she came down and saw Heinrich in the parlour, her courage failed her.

After just a short time in the parlour, her head started to ache, probably from the sour, stale smell in the room that hadn't been aired in a long time. She didn't like the parlour anyway – it was too gloomy and formal, with old furniture dating back to Heinrich and Frieda's parents.

Hanging on the walls in cramped rows were yellowing, faded photographs of relatives she'd never met. There was an upright cabinet ornamented with shells, crocheted covers on the armrests of the chairs, fixed with pins that pricked when you leaned back, and faded wallpaper that took away any cosiness the room might have offered.

Now for the first time in ages, the window shutters were open and a fine layer of dust covering the furniture and pictures was visible in the daylight.

None of this bothered Heinrich. He was loafing comfortably on the sofa, his long legs protruding far over the armrest, smoking one of his Russian cigarettes with the long cardboard tubes. Kathrin never liked it when he smoked in the parlour; her mother had told her that tobacco smoke turned the curtains yellow. She remembered all too well the endless nagging and quarrels between her parents over the curtains and in the first years of her marriage, she had often asked Heinrich not to smoke in the parlour.

Now none of it mattered to her. Neither her husband nor his curtains. Sometimes she even felt that she was just visiting and that her stay in Heinrich Marten's house must soon end. Then she would leave, but she didn't know where, only that she wouldn't go alone. She now thought of herself and Alexei as 'we', as if he were a part of her, and she would die if he left her.

She sat down in the green armchair, very stiffly, because of the pins in the crocheted covers, then cautiously asked Heinrich whether he had any plans for the evening.

His head lolled in her direction. 'Maybe I'll drop by the inn. What do you think?'

Perhaps he'd expected her to object. But he was disappointed when she promptly agreed, sounding relieved and almost too eager.

Kathrin had always been disgusted on Saturday evenings when he'd come home drunk and had thrown himself onto the bed, fully clothed, snoring before his head hit the pillow. Today she hoped he would get drunk. She knew how they treated soldiers on leave at the inn: the innkeeper always had a bottle of good, aged Cognac under the counter for such occasions.

Kathrin cheered right up. She leapt to her feet and ran into the kitchen, where Frieda was sweating over the oven. Together they prepared dinner, rich and greasy, just as Heinrich liked it.

II.

As daylight was fading, Heinrich left the house. Kathrin breathed out. A sudden wave of exhaustion came over her, and her limbs went slack: her pretence of calm and ease had taken more out of her than she realized.

She went up to bed very early. On the stairs, she paused, wanting to see Alexei. Her longing to be near him and hear some comforting words hurt her like a physical pain. But she didn't turn around. Leaning heavily on the banister, she dragged herself up the stairs, one step at a time.

She stood at the bedroom window. The sun had already gone down, and a few small clouds, tinged with a last shimmer of red, were scudding quickly across the horizon as it grew pale. The woods sank into the violet dusk, and the light in the sky was snuffed out.

Blue shadows sloped up the walls, blurring every edge and corner of the room. Kathrin sat motionless on her bed, her hands stretched out flat on her lap. They lay there still and pale, seeming not to belong to her. The fresh sheets gave off a hint of lavender; like her mother, Kathrin always placed a couple of dried sprigs among the linen in the drawers.

Kathrin didn't undress. She waited.

She sat up, startled, having fallen asleep after all. Now it was quiet in the house, while outside the crickets chirped and the poplar leaves rustled. Moonlight filled the bedroom. Kathrin sat up and got a shock. On the bright floorboards lay the shadow of a black cross, its vertical and horizontal sections in sharp relief, like a cross on a grave.

All at once, she knew that nothing, absolutely nothing, had been gained; there would be no respite or running away. She listened out in the night. The farm gate clunked shut, echoing dully like a shot in the nearby wood.

Kathrin jumped up, looked at the door, stricken, then ran to the window. She clung to the crossbar of the window and stared out into the garden, which seemed very far below her.

Steps pounded up the stairs; she counted each stair according to the noise it made.

The third creaked, the fifth too. Two left, now one . . .

Kathrin closed her eyes. She tried to think of Alexei, but his figure was blurred and his face seemed hidden in a wall of fog, grey on grey.

She straightened up, her shoulders pushed back. The fog dissolved.

A heavy body thudded against the post, shoving the door open. Her husband stood there on the threshold, his face red, his lids swollen, and his hair stuck in messy strands across his forehead, matte and slick with sweat.

A look from his glittering, watery eyes passed over her.

She went white and bit her lip.

Pale moonlight was falling through the hatch in the roof. The Russian was lying in the straw, his knees drawn up to his body. He wasn't asleep.

He started when he heard the clunk of the farm gate. *Katyusha!* he thought *Katyusha!*

Such a wild anger seized him that he broke out in a cold sweat, and his heart tightened. He knew that she needed him, especially now, and that he had to go to her and protect her.

Alexei jumped up and stood with his hands raised and neck craned in the pale light, the dark joists forming crosses over his head in the dark. Painfully tense, he listened out. No noise came from the house.

The animals and trees were quiet that night.

Suddenly, the bated silence was split by a plaintive cry, short and sharp like a night bird's call. Alexei lunged forward. 'Kathrin!' he yelled. He threw himself against the door, which juddered from the impact of his sturdy body. He hammered his fists against the wood, shouting.

The farm and the whole world woke up: the dog yowled and pulled on its chain, the poplars and the woods rustled, the lake churned, and the stars teemed in the sky – but none of the uproar could drown out the short, plaintive wail that hung trembling above the commotion.

Alexei crouched to his knees and pressed his head against the doorpost. *Kathrin, I'm with you – they've locked me in here like an animal, like a rabid dog, but I'm with you, now and for ever. Do you hear me, Kathrin? Do – you – hear – me?*

No answer. No more cries, not a sound could be heard on the farm or from the house.

The light trickled in grudgingly, the moon wandered across the sky, and the joists sank back into darkness. Deep shadows slunk out of the corners towards the Russian.

Kathrin was no longer afraid. To protect herself, she held an arm over her head but she didn't cry out as the hands beat her chest and body.

'You tart,' gurgled her husband. 'You piece of filth.' He hit her with his fist, and she staggered.

'Whore, damn you!' He pulled her arm away from her face. 'You Russian whore!'

She let out a cry, short and sharp like a night bird. One of her eyebrows had burst open, and blood, warm and sticky, was trickling down her cheek. She clapped both hands to her face, saw the blood on her fingers and fell. The back of her head hit the edge of the bed.

Heinrich turned to stone. His wife was lying on the floor, a pitiful little bundle, her arms flung to each side as if she were crucified on the shadow of the window's crossbar.

'Kathrin!' he cried, and through the red fug of his drunkenness and anger that dulled his eyes and brain, a bright, paralysing shock flashed through him: *You've killed her!*

He leaned over her, breathing heavily. A thin trickle of blood ran across her cheek to her ear and seeped into her fair hair. He lay a hand on her chest, felt her heartbeat and straightened up. A daft smile flickered across his bloated face. 'She's alive, thank God.'

He blundered his way down the stairs, fetched some water and clumsily tried to pour some into her mouth. She snapped open her eyes and stammered, 'It's not true. Nothing is going on with him – he doesn't know anything. I swear—'

'I know, I know,' said Heinrich desperately. He picked her up and carried her to bed. 'It's not true,' she whispered. 'I swear—' Heinrich sat down on the edge of the bed, his skull throbbing, and he said, 'No, it's not true. I know it's not.'

'I swear—'

'I believe you, Kathrin. Just go to sleep, Kathrin. Tomorrow—'

His head toppled forward, and he fell asleep, snoring, his mouth ajar.

'He doesn't know anything,' whispered Kathrin. 'I swear. Oh, Alexei . . .'

Heinrich Marten sat huddled on the trough near the pump, blinking with bleary eyes at the sun. His head pounded. What a way to wake up! Such terrible dreams last night. And the worst part wasn't even the dream, but reality. Kathrin walked about the house, silent and pale, a plaster over her right eye, doing nothing, saying nothing, just walking about the house, up and down the stairs, as if deranged.

He'd stopped her in the entrance hall that morning and murmured, 'Sorry, Kathrin—'

She'd only smiled, as if she didn't know him, and had carried on past him.

He placed a hand on his forehead, brooding. How had it come to this? How could he have hit her? He, who'd always said he'd could never beat his wife?

The bloody booze!

When he'd gone to the inn, he'd been shipshape. Ten, maybe twelve farmers had been sitting there, mostly the older ones, and some young lads too.

They'd welcomed him, one loudly, shaking his hand, another quietly, with just a short nod or a terse word. The innkeeper had fetched a bottle from under the counter – fine, aged Cognac – and Heinrich had bought one round, then another. They drank, and he told stories about life on the front, and they told stories about work, the village and the harvest. Things got heated, they got louder, and the innkeeper kept steadily filling their glasses – my God, what a Cognac! A fine vintage!

Then Anders had arrived, the old pot-stirrer. Friendly as you like, he'd asked after Kathrin and what kind of welcome Heinrich had been given at home. Heinrich was taken aback. There was that tone again, that thinly veiled scorn, like in the afternoon. That rascal, damn him!

He'd flared up: what did he mean by all his stupid questions? The farmers grinned.

He became agitated, then angry. What business of theirs was Kathrin? What the hell was going on? The farmers kept on grinning, their mouths wide.

He stood up and steadied himself on the table, looking from one face to another; his expression wiped the grins off their faces.

If only he'd left right then! But no, he was vexed that his wife was up to something he didn't know about. He shot Anders a direct question. But the old man backtracked. He knew nothing and had said nothing.

'It's just women's gossip,' one chipped in.

'What kind of women's gossip?' asked Heinrich, with the insistence of a drunk, not letting up, thundering and shouting. Then it all came out. God, well, you know, women and their chatter, a load of old rubbish, probably – the village was full of it. Don't upset yourself, Heinrich, it's just a rumour . . .

'What kind of rumour?' he yelled. 'I want to hear the rumour, I want names!' He yanked Anders' sleeve. 'You're my witness, Anders, you started all this, you've seen something—'

'Now I'm for it,' murmured the old man. 'Now I've really put my foot in it because of that *Panje*.'

Heinrich stammered. '*Panje*—? He first had to translate the world. *Panje* – slang for Russian . . . 'The Russki . . .?' He fell back on a chair, flustered. 'What are you saying? . . . Kathrin – with that stupid oaf? He can't even speak three words of German. That's impossible . . .'

He sat hunched over the table, gaping like a blind man at the stained tabletop.

The others tried to reassure him. A few of them really wanted to calm him down, but Anders and a couple of the young lads made a game out of stirring him up even more with their snide remarks and pretend commiserations.

Heinrich drank three strong shots of schnapps, much too quickly. Out of nowhere, a cry came from the door, a young, strident voice: 'Heil Hitler!'

'Heil Hitler!' said the innkeeper, and the others muttered unintelligibly. Heinrich didn't look up.

Horst Lange, the overseer, sat down with them at the table, laughing. 'So, lads, what's all this then? Someone died?'

He cut a striking, youthful figure, always in jackboots and brown trousers, his 'candy' or Party badge on his lapel, and big words about the Führer and the Fatherland on his lips.

The old farmers made fun of him and sometimes even threw insults at him, but when he sat down with them, they hushed up.

The overseer had long since had eyes and ears everywhere, believing he was officially entitled to know everything that went on in the village. But some things remained hidden from him, things like black-market slaughters and all kinds of gossip that people thought a man with a piece of candy on his lapel didn't need to know. He had a hunch this went on and that's why he often sat in the inn and snooped on conversations between Anders and Weckerling and Franke, and all the other farmers whose word in the village was respected.

Horst Lange noticed straight away that something was up. Marten was staring forwards like an idiot, his eyes unfocused, and the men around him had all put on uninterested expressions. What kind of shenanigans were they up to now? And as he was officially entitled to ask, Horst Lange did just that, in a stern voice, without beating around the bush.

The innkeeper vanished without a word into the back room.

The men and lads slouched back, their blank faces alternately wrinkled and smooth, not saying a word in the blue fug of cigarette smoke.

Old Anders said evenly, 'People say that the wife of this one here', and now he jabbed his thumb at Heinrich Marten, 'is having it off with her prisoner.'

Heinrich Marten flinched. In a flash and with surprising clarity, he thought: *The old man doesn't care what happens. He's already up to his ears in misery. And he just wants to drag everyone else down into the dirt, because his Grete is already in it . . .*

He looked at the farmers' overseer. Lange had leapt up from his chair, his young, already too harsh face flushed, and had started shouting into the deep silence. It took Heinrich quite a long time to realize why the man was shouting that way. Slowly, he stood up, leaned across the table, grabbed Lange by the lapels and said quietly, with effort, 'What are you shouting about? You want to report Kathrin? Report my wife, is that it? Because a few idiots here are babbling about her having it off with the Russian, is that it?' He suddenly grew loud. and his voice cracked, just as everything – the inn and the table, the men and this idiotic fellow in jackboots who he'd never been able to stand – seemed to whirl around his head. 'My wife is none of your goddamned business! That's between me and her – and if you go sticking your nose into my affairs, I'll beat you to a pulp, get it?'

The other, pale and red, tried unsuccessfully to shake off the drunken man, tried to stand up to his booming voice, yapping something in fear and anger about 'being his superior'.

'Nothing is going on between my wife and the Russki, and there'll never be anything going on between her and that sort either. You can bet your life on it! And shut your gob about being my superior. I'm a soldier! Fighting on the front! Got the Iron Cross – you see that? And you? Kicking your heels at home, a young lad, with no idea what war's like, snooping around after a soldier's wife – you pig!' And he shoved Lange in the chest, who then staggered, only managing with an effort to stay upright.

Two or three men jumped up, but Heinrich brushed them off with a broad sweep of his arm. 'Shut your mouths, all of you! Accuse an innocent woman, would you? With a Russian – ha! – of all people! Throw muck at your own walls, there's enough of it!' He chucked a couple of banknotes onto the table. He swayed his way to the door, stumbling at the step. The night air cooled his heated face, and he managed to walk a straight path home.

Something like satisfaction came over him. He'd shown them! But deep inside, he was eaten up by doubt. What if they were right? What if there were some truth to their gossip? What if he'd made a fool of himself in front of the whole village?

When he finally entered the bedroom, Kathrin was standing by the window. She was so upright, so unafraid, so different from her usual self, and the look on her face stirred up his emotions so much that he'd lashed out indiscriminately in a fit of senseless rage.

Damned booze!

Heinrich pushed himself up from the trough and went into the house. In the entrance hall, he managed to catch hold of Kathrin, grabbing her arm and gabbling, 'I believe you, Kathrin. With a Russian? Rubbish. It's all rubbish. And the other thing,' he added, more quietly, 'I don't know what came over me. Forget it, Kathrin.'

'No,' she said. She was much smaller than him, but in his desperate position, he felt as if he were looking up to her. She saw the fatuous look in his round, brown eyes and added, 'It's all right, Heinrich. Don't worry about me. Everything's fine.' She calmly freed herself from his grip. Her face wasn't even angry. In fact, she looked quite friendly. But as she pulled away from him, Heinrich instantly knew that things between them were over.

He turned away, his head hanging, his broad back hunched over, and walked through the entrance hall like an old man.

Heinrich had never loved his wife with a passion. He'd accepted her as she was, in all her dowdiness, because she came with a few acres of land that he couldn't have got his hands on otherwise, no matter how hard he tried. But he'd been good to her – in his own way. He'd got used to her in their five years of marriage and needed the bit of warmth she could give him. And now he suddenly realized that in those five years he hadn't got to know her at all. Her presence was like his daily bread. Cherries were tastier, of course, and he'd picked some, but they weren't for the long run. He couldn't live off cherries alone; he'd always need bread, and bread kept him from overeating. Everything else was just a side dish.

That evening they went up to the bedroom together. Kathrin made the bed, but her husband wordlessly took his pillow and settled downstairs on the sofa in the parlour. He'd had to sleep on his own without the warmth of a woman for so many nights that he soon fell asleep that night too. And his sleep was so deep and sound that he didn't hear Kathrin coming into the parlour that night and sitting for a long time in the dark on one of the armchairs, very stiffly because of the pins keeping the lace covers in place.

Kathrin must have sat by her sleeping husband for an hour, listening to his noisy breathing and the creaking of the steel springs as he tossed around on the old sofa.

When Kathrin eventually went back up to the bedroom, she was no longer afraid of Heinrich Marten and didn't hate him either. He was now very far away from her, a wanderer on a country road that narrowed on the distant horizon into one single point where he vanished, never to be seen again.

On the last day of his leave, the couple were very polite to each other. Heinrich busied himself with work on the farm, as there were a thousand little things to repair that hadn't been taken care of recently. And Kathrin attended to him like a guest, not one who was especially dear to her nor one who had outstayed his welcome.

That evening, Heinrich had to leave.

He was wearing his grey uniform again. In his jacket, he looked even bulkier, but his face was drawn and worried when he reached out his hand to Kathrin. 'Until next time,' he said, as if he didn't believe there would be a next time.

'You're not coming with me to the station?' he asked, trying to keep his voice steady and casual.

'No,' said Kathrin. All the same, it had been five years, and Heinrich wasn't as loud, strong and healthy as he used to be: that's why he pulled his young wife up onto her tiptoes and kissed her on the mouth. She closed her eyes as he did so, and so she didn't see the painful shock in his eyes but felt it in his embrace.

Heinrich had got as far as the neighbour's farm when he turned around after all. Kathrin raised her hand and waved to him with a handkerchief. Heinrich gave a last wave and then he vanished from his wife's view as he rounded the bend in the path.

Kathrin lowered her raised arm.

The man in uniform walked back along the path he'd come down two days earlier and didn't look back. Behind him, the village sank into the arms of the wood; for a few minutes, the tip of the church steeple stood blinking against the red sky, and then it too went out.

It was a mild evening, but the man plodded more arduously along the dusty road than when he'd arrived in the glare of the midday sun. It was as if the farm had been razed to the ground behind him; it dawned on him that it was the last time he'd stand with Kathrin beneath the archway of the gate.

He wasn't afraid of the trenches, the rattling tanks or the cries of the wounded; he didn't long to return to his village either. On his mouth, he could still feel Kathrin's lips and for the first time in his loud, robust, active life, he strayed from the straight path in his thoughts. He was now stuck in a murky thicket of pointless brooding, not knowing which way was forward and which back.

On the train, he ran into a couple of fellow soldiers, and one had a bottle of schnapps. When they started passing the bottle around, Heinrich was still on the lonely country road between his village and the town in his thoughts. But then one of them pulled skat cards out of his pocket and they set up a game on a knapsack. The bottle went around, the soldiers laughed and told jokes, and life became easier again. Heinrich told a smutty joke, and the others slapped their thighs. He slipped straight back into his soldier's life, grumbling about his commanding officer, as he took a long swig from the bottle – what the hell, here today, gone tomorrow! That night he slept almost as comfortably on the hard wooden bench of the wagon as he had the day before on the parlour sofa.

12.

Kathrin leaned against the poplar tree. While keeping her eyes on the bend in the road, she interlaced her fingers behind her back, feeling the smooth, grey bark of the familiar tree. Her husband had disappeared. And their farewell had been final, as if what divided them wasn't a few kilometres of country road, but life's last three feet of earth.

She turned around. Alexei was standing at the fence behind her. She didn't wave, nod or smile; she just looked at him, an expression of liberation on her face.

Kathrin and Alexei walked along the narrow strip at the edge of the field, walled in by golden wheat to their left and right, and then continued down to the lake. A sparse copse of slim pines separated the fields from the gently sloping shore, their bark the colour of fire. A cool breeze wafted across the lake, bringing with it an acrid whiff of fish, rotting arrowhead and waterweed.

They sat down on the loose, white sand near the belt of reeds surrounding the lake, which was only broken here and there by the narrow gaps people walked through to get into the water.

The last rays of the sun formed an arc over the lake. Alexei reached for Kathrin's hand, and they listened to the slapping of waves. Frogs croaked idly, and a fish flicked out of the water.

Kathrin said quietly, 'I often sat here as a young girl,

you know. This is how I imagined paradise – so tranquil, the animals living side by side in peace, speaking to us people . . .' She fell silent. As the sun went down, the golden arc of light sank. Kathrin, lost in thought, looked down at her lap and said bitterly, 'But everything was different back then. There's no peace in the world any more, not here or anywhere. We don't understand the language of animals any more, and they don't live side by side in peace. The old pike is in the reeds, lying in wait for his prey. The frogs snap up flies, and the birds dive into swarms of mosquitoes to pick them off. Everyone's fighting each other, and the strong devour the weak. Ach, paradise – where's a bit of peace in the world, Alexei?'

'What about people!' Alexei said.

'People . . .' Kathrin repeated thinly, 'they're the worst. Wars are going on everywhere, people are devouring each other, like packs of wolves. Parents are selling their children. When my father died, I didn't even cry.'

The sky was like green silk, and a velvety grey glaze covered the lake.

Alexei put his arm around Kathrin's shoulders. 'You have to believe in people, Katja,' he said. 'People are good, and there will be peace. People have longed for paradise for thousands of years and have gone through dirt and blood for it. We'll change the world. Wars don't have to come and go like summer and winter. One day, there'll be no more poverty, no enemies or hatred. People will live in peace, and everyone will have enough to eat and be happy. Then we can dream again, Kathrin . . .'

'We won't live to see that, Alexei.'

'The people born after us will. My country has made a start, and the world will follow.'

'But your country is fighting the war too. You kill—'

'We kill to win back life.'

'That's difficult to understand, Alexei.'

'We were forced to go to war. We were invaded and had to defend ourselves. We couldn't just stand back and let them rob us of everything. You understand that, don't you?'

'If only what you're saying were true, Alexei. I'd so like to believe you . . .' She turned her head towards him. 'You say you've started to do everything differently in Russia – you've collectivized your land, and have started to create a new kind of person. But we're in Germany.'

The lake shimmered dully in soft pastel colours. As if drawn in black ink on violet silk paper, the silhouettes of the reeds stood out against the sky.

'For as long as I'm listening to you, I'm not scared or doubtful,' Kathrin said. 'If you just stay with me . . .'

Alexei took her head in both hands and kissed her on the mouth and eyes. She returned his kiss, and her heart was beating so fast and hard that she thought he must be able to hear it. His hand slid from her shoulder and cupped her breast. For a moment, Kathrin relaxed in his embrace, then she pushed him away.

Breathlessly, she said, 'But what about when the war ends – what will happen to us?'

Alexei turned his head away. 'I don't know,' he said sullenly.

'You'll go back to your village. But what about me?'

Alexei grasped her hair and pulled her to his chest. She couldn't bear to see his unhappy face, and now all she could hear was his voice, trying to reassure her. 'I'll take you with me. Of course I will. We'll go back to Ukraine and build ourselves a new house—'

Kathrin smiled and said quietly, with her eyes closed, 'Once upon a time, there was a man and a woman. They had a house and a garden and in it bloomed a thousand sunflowers. They worked and tilled the land and loved each other to the end of their days . . .' She opened her eyes. 'That's a fairy tale, Alexei. The kind of story you tell at bedtime. Even you don't believe it.'

He didn't reply.

The water was almost black by now. Kathrin pointed to the lake shore, where a couple of water lilies were floating in the middle of dark round leaves. 'They look like white birds at night.'

'Shall I fetch you some?'

'Oh, no,' Kathrin said hastily, 'there are sharp dips everywhere and weeds that can tangle you up. Then you can never get out. Last year, a boy drowned just a few metres from the shore.'

Alexei laughed. 'You think I don't dare?' He'd already slipped off his wooden clogs and was rolling up his trousers. He walked across the loose, damp sand and a few steps into the water until it reached his knees, then took one more step, and plunged in up to his hip. He bent over the tangle of plate-sized leaves, deftly breaking off a couple of water lilies.

He waded back. Kathrin raised her arms when he tried to give them to her. 'Don't, Alexei, they're flowers for the dead, you mustn't give them to me.'

Smiling, he shook his head. 'How can you say such a thing – flowers for the dead? . . . Just look at how lovely they are.' They had closed up for the night, and their milky-white, silky petals tightly overlapped with a hint of pink here and there.

Kathrin squatted on the shore and reluctantly took the long-stemmed flowers. Then she shrank back and cried, 'But everyone says they cause bad luck! If you pick them, you die in the same year!'

She jumped to her feet and flung the water lilies back into the water in a sweeping arc. They drifted off, bobbing slightly on the waves.

Kathrin was shivering when Alexei looked at her. The water lapped at his feet. He came ashore and flung his arms around her. Against his chest, she whispered, 'If anything bad happened to you, Alexei, I'd die.'

He bent down towards her. She stroked his damp hair, and his breath brushed her cheeks. Abruptly, she threw her arms around his neck and said in a throttled voice, 'Kiss me, hold me tight, you're still here now, I have to feel that you're still here.'

He kissed her, wildly and in desperation. 'Katyusha, my dove . . .'

In the sky above them, the blue night sky, she saw the first flickering star. 'Tell me you love me. Say it in your language.'

Falteringly, Alexei said, *'Ya tebya lyublyu.'*

13.

One evening, Kathrin took the prisoner into the kitchen. He'd asked so often to listen to the radio that she could no longer refuse him. She said, 'It's dangerous, Alexei. If Frieda discovers you're in the house at night . . . Your soldiers are making advances – that's what you wanted to know, right?'

The kitchen window was open, and the blue-and-white gingham curtains billowed. Kathrin closed the window and rolled down the blackout cloth. When she lit the hanging lamp above the table, Alexei saw that she was shaking with nerves.

'You have to be very quiet,' she said. 'Frieda's room is above the kitchen.'

The small Volksempfänger radio, with its swastikas embossed beside the tuning panel, was on the dresser next to the bread box. Alexei bent down and bit his bottom lip when he caught sight of the eagle clutching a swastika in its claws. Kathrin watched him very nervously and said, 'I could have told you what they're saying on the news.'

She realized he wasn't listening to her. His expression was rigid with concentration as he turned the dial. Snatches of music came from the speakers, then an air-raid warning, some military songs and operettas; a voice announced: '. . . in the name of the *Volk*, those sentenced to death are Karl Wachsmuth, Lieselotte Grabow, Rudolf Stegmann . . .'

They looked at each other, both of them now pale. Alexei hesitated for a moment then carried on turning the dial.

The sound crackled and whined like a snowstorm and suddenly there was silence. From far away came the first bars of a song that Alexei hummed to himself.

'God, what are you doing? What are you listening to?' cried Kathrin.

A quiet voice, as distant as if from another planet, said: '*Govorit Moskva . . . Govorit Moskva*' – Moscow speaking. Alexei grasped the radio with both hands and pressed his ear to the loudspeaker.

Kathrin lunged at him. 'You're going to get both of us killed.'

Alexei turned, and his expression was shaken yet happy. He crouched down and held Kathrin's hips. 'My country,' he said breathlessly. '*Slyshyesh*, d'you hear? My comrades . . .' He spoke to her in a rush, and she didn't understand. All of a sudden, he'd forgotten his German and out of his mouth came a barrage of Russian words.

Kathrin slowly pulled away. She looked at him; the person closest to her had suddenly become a stranger.

The loudspeaker began crackling and whistling. Alexei let Kathrin go and desperately tried to find the radio station again.

'Alexei,' said Kathrin. 'Alyosha . . .' She waited, but he'd forgotten her. At a loss, she gazed around the kitchen, at the photograph of Heinrich on the wall, laughing in his uniform, and then back to Alexei. His head was leaning against the dresser, and he was listening intently to the Russian voice, the sound of his country, which was travelling thousands of kilometres to where he stood in the kitchen of a German farmhouse. And Kathrin understood that there was something beyond this farm, something bigger and stronger than her love, an unbreakable bond that joined Alexei to his country.

She tiptoed back to the door and said, more to herself than the Russian, 'I'll go and check—'

Alexei, hunched over the dresser, had rested his head on his arms. He was crying.

14.

The air over the harvested field flickered with heat.

The sky, leaden grey, trembled where it met the ground, while the sun shot white-hot arrows almost vertically onto the three people below. The horses pulled sluggishly, and the wheels of the hay cart ground the dust between rows of stubble.

Frieda, her skirt hoisted high above her round calves, was passing up sheaf after sheaf with a strength and agility that matched Alexei's, while Kathrin, breathing hard, could barely keep up. She was standing on the cart, and her dusty grey undershirt – her blouse had long since been cast aside – exposed her round, tanned shoulders, arms and neck. She didn't even have time to wipe the sweat from her face and now it burned on her skin, raw and scratched by thousands of slender bristles from the awns swirling through the air.

She choked back the nausea that was being churned up by an iron fist painfully cramping her stomach. She didn't know whether it was the heat, the dreadful humidity that made her vest stick to her back or her raging hunger. That morning, she hadn't been able to eat anything; bread repulsed her, and she hadn't been able to hold down sausage for a few days now. She'd had to make do with a few sips of malt coffee.

Her movements slowed down because she could barely raise her slack arms. She saw Alexei's concerned look as he passed her up a sheaf and she gathered the last of her strength so as not to worry him. If she could only rest for an hour, or even for just a half or quarter of an hour, if she could only lie in the shade and catch her breath . . . oh, but the line of sheaves was still so long and Frieda wasn't likely to take a break. She could work like a horse, was strong and healthy, and anyway, the wheat had to come in because a storm was expected that evening.

Kathrin lurched, and the field began to spin before her eyes, turning faster and faster in a mad dance. She keeled forward and would have fallen off the cart, had Alexei, who wasn't letting her out of his sight for a minute, not stretched out his arms and caught her.

From far away, Frieda's voice boomed in Kathrin's ear. She didn't understand the words but squirmed out of the Russian's arms. Even in her swoon, she didn't forget her sister-in-law's watchfulness, so deeply etched into her mind was the constant danger. Like a drunk, she staggered a few small steps across the stiff stubble, not feeling the pain under her bare feet. She made it to the edge of the field and then threw up.

Frieda ran over to her at an ungainly trot, having got a fright. She was shocked to see Kathrin's tear-stained face, twitching in pain.

'Now, now, what's the matter? You're not getting sick, are you? In the middle of the harvest?' Kathrin shook her head feebly.

'Oh God, that's just what we need,' griped her sister-in-law. 'The barley has to be brought in, and we're barely keeping up as it is.' She pushed her rough hand under Kathrin's head. Frieda's hot breath and the sour smell of sweat hit Kathrin in the face. She struggled into a sitting position and glanced at Alexei. He was standing a little way off, his arms hanging by his sides, his face quite grey with panic.

'It's nothing,' whispered Kathrin. 'I feel better already.' Without help, she stood up. Alexei instinctively stretched out his arms. But Kathrin was already up, swaying slightly, and she smiled at him. 'Really, I'm much better.'

Then she spun around.

'Heil Hitler!' belted the strident voice of the farmers' overseer. His arm was raised in salute as he stood to attention, dressed in brown stormtrooper trousers and jackboots despite the heat. The Party badge on his shirt collar glinted like a wicked spider; the farmers joked that he probably even pinned it to his nightgown.

'What's going on?' He spoke curtly and sternly, as he liked to act assertive in front of women – he knew they bore a grudge against him.

'Nowt's going on,' thundered Frieda. She couldn't stand Lange, a young, healthy man who loafed around at home and who'd never had a taste of the front. 'Touch of sunstroke,' she added and turned her back to him, hoisting her skirt higher at the back so that it looked like a bawdy provocation.

Lange glanced swiftly back and forth between Alexei and Kathrin: he held his nose aloft like a hunting dog catching a scent. For weeks now, he'd been skulking around the Martens' farmhouse, still bothered by the events of that evening at the inn, unable to forget that Heinrich Marten had gone for his throat in front of all the farmers. He didn't believe the man's enraged claims that nothing was going on between his wife and the prisoner. Besides, it was his official duty to be suspicious!

He would not tolerate any shenanigans in his village! A German woman, carrying on with a foreigner – and one of inferior race, to boot – right under his nose? *Not in my backyard, sweetie*, he thought.

He sneaked a look at the Russian. True, he was blond and blue-eyed – northern stock, who knew where from? – but the high cheekbones and round head revealed Slavic roots. Lange was against putting Bolsheviks to work on farms in the first place. They only caused trouble, the lot of them. Not long ago, one in the neighbouring village had escaped. He hadn't made it far, but that careless episode had cost the other farmers' overseer his position.

No, he couldn't just remove the Martens' prisoner for no obvious reason, especially during the harvest. That fat bint Frieda would scratch his eyes out, and without a man to help on the farm, the grain delivery would be in a sorry mess.

Frieda glanced back over her shoulder at him. 'Hey, why are you still standing around here?' she yelled over to him. 'If you need something to do, just say so. We could use some help.'

'Shut it!' Lange bawled. These big-mouthed women! He shouted back, 'I wanted a word with you about the delivery—'

'Gone mad, have you?' Frieda barked back. 'Our sort has other things to do at harvest time.'

'Then I'll be dropping by again shortly.' With this, his retreat was covered, and he sloped off, disgruntled and annoyed. The tone these women had taken up since their men had left home! Yet they had brains the size of peas and didn't get that the work carried out in the homeland was just as important as the work on the front. After all, supplies had to be secured and replenished, and that's why the Party needed men like him at the rear.

He sneaked a glance back. Kathrin Martens and the prisoner were walking slowly over the field to the hay cart, a few metres apart, like two strangers. He hadn't spotted a familiar gesture or a secret look between them. Still, he thought to himself, the local gossip he'd chanced to overhear couldn't all be made up. He would keep his eyes peeled! Then he whistled a few bars of his favourite song, very loudly and almost in tune: 'It'll pass, one day it'll all be over . . .'

Why does that fella always have to pry around here? Frieda thought. *Sticks his nose into everything, that know-it-all . . .* She called over to Kathrin. 'Go to Trude Meinhardt's this evening, get her to prescribe you something. We're taking in the barley tomorrow, and I need you back on your feet.'

Kathrin nodded absently. Prescribe something? A few drops or tablets weren't going to help. She struggled to climb back up on the cart and started to layer the sheaves again. Oh, she was too slow! At that, Frieda threw down her pitchfork and clambered up on the cart herself, scolding and panting. Kathrin, scrap of a thing that she was, had done enough! Frieda shoved her to one side, hollering something about 'resting' and 'sitting down', and Kathrin stepped gratefully aside.

Haltingly, the cart moved forward. Grey dust rose. Then the horses came to a standstill again, their heads hanging in the glare of the sun.

Kathrin sat down on the path in the scant shade of the scrubby furze. Only a few days earlier, she'd come here with Alexei when the crops had been swaying softly in the evening breeze. They'd lain in the arms of the field and looked up at the starry sky, and Alexei's hands had been warm and tender like the nights.

Now the barren field of stubble stretched out in front of her, like the huge hand of an old man, bare and wilting.

Kathrin closed her eyes, shivering in the midday heat.

Kathrin sat on the pallet in the sickroom, her hands hugging her knees, thinking it was pointless to have come here, knowing that lying wouldn't help and that the truth would only make everything worse.

Trude Meinhardt sat opposite her, looking very official in her starched white apron under the weak glow from the single lightbulb that swung from the ceiling. Her dark eyes were keenly inspecting the young woman's face, but Kathrin had shut herself off, her lips pressed into a line of helpless defiance.

'No appetite?'

'No.'

'You feel sick in the mornings? Have to vomit frequently?'

Hesitation.

'Yes.'

Trude slowly crossed the room to the doctor's cabinet and took out a long blue packet. She spoke to the wall. 'You can take this for the sickness. Whether it'll help, I don't know.' She weighed the packet in her hand. Suddenly she spun around, her eyes glittering, and shouted fiercely, 'Why are you lying to me, Kathrin? Do you think I'm so stupid that I don't know what's going on with you?' Then, quietly, 'I've given birth to two children—'

Soundlessly, Kathrin crumpled forward. Her thin shoulders trembled.

Trude yanked her upright. 'So, it's true! Oh God, oh God!' She searched Kathrin's face, but the younger woman had borne too much over the past few years and had learned how to control herself; she could stop the fear in her heart from showing in her face. When she spoke, though, Trude could immediately tell how deeply she was suffering.

'What should I do, Trude? I felt it but didn't want to believe it. It's wonderful. And it's terrible. A child – oh, Trude, I've always wanted a child.' Then she cried out, 'But they'll take it away from me, they'll beat me, and I won't be allowed to give birth—' Her voice splintered.

Trude went over to the window. Dark clouds were covering the stars. In the distance, sheet lightning flashed and thunder rolled. *A storm's brewing*, she thought.

'Help me,' Kathrin whimpered.

Trude came over to Kathrin and took her hands in her own. She whispered quickly, avoiding Kathrin's pleading eyes. 'There's only one way – if no one knows yet . . . I've never done such a thing but I think I could—'

Kathrin placed a hand on her belly. It wasn't even murder. The creature hadn't even begun to live yet and it would feel no pain.

'You can only be in the beginning of your second month,' said Trude. 'It's not even a proper child yet – no shape, no eyes, ears or limbs, and it still can't feel either.'

. . . *'Katyusha,' Alexei presses his lips to her mouth and his hands are as warm as the night by the lake. Water lilies bob on the waves, and a bird chirps sleepily. Kathrin looks up into the sky and the stars become one with the eyes of the man very close above her face.*

'There's no point in carrying the child to full term,'

Trude was saying. 'These are terrible times – we don't know what'll happen to us tomorrow, when this war will end or if we'll even live to see it.'

'What about people!' says Alexei. 'One day, there'll be no more poverty, no enemies or hatred. People will live in peace, and everyone will have enough to eat and be happy. We have to believe in that and fight for it, Kathrin, then we can dream again . . .'

Kathrin lifted her head. 'I want to keep the child,' she said.

Trude stood up and smoothed out her white apron with both hands.

'Forget what I said.' Her thin, grave face was flushed red.

'It's Alexei's child.' Kathrin smiled shyly. 'He says that one day, there'll be peace in the world. The people born after us will live to see it—'

'I wish you all the luck in the world,' Trude said. 'Keep your child – perhaps he or she will really live to see everything – peace, calm, safety . . . people being kind to one another. Oh, Kathrin . . .'

She began to cry.

Kathrin slipped out of the sickroom. Outside, the approaching storm engulfed her. The trees bent over, creaking, their leaves shuddering. A tongue of glaring lightning flashed through the night, and the thunder rumbled even louder. Now the first heavy raindrops started to fall, and the earth and air smelled damp and acrid.

Kathrin ran along the village road. The rain started falling more heavily and she gladly let it cover her face and arms. By the time she reached the farm, she was drenched to the skin.

'Just look at you!' Frieda cried. 'Change your clothes, you'll catch your death.'

Kathrin panicked. She might catch a cold and it could harm her child. She tore off her wet things and rubbed herself dry with a vigour that made Frieda cry out, 'Well, it's not as bad as all that! What did Meinhardt say?'

'Nothing in particular. I'm not really sick, just a bit poorly,' Kathrin murmured into the towel. Only now did she realize that she'd forgotten to take the tablets. But she wouldn't go back and fetch them because those kinds of medicines always contained toxic ingredients, and they would harm her child. It was just a bit of queasiness, that was all.

She almost felt like laughing when Frieda fetched her own woollen housecoat – a shapeless, wide thing that draped loosely around her gaunt limbs – and forced Kathrin into it, saying, 'Just don't get ill, we have to fetch in the barley tomorrow.'

August passed.

Whatever Kathrin said or did, her thoughts were always on the child growing inside her. She often laughed and sang, was friendlier than ever to the women in the village and couldn't walk past playing children without stopping.

Whenever she leaned over a pram, the mother blushed with pride. With astonished delight, Kathrin inspected tiny mother-of-pearl nails on little round hands.

The work during harvest time was hard. Her back often ached, but she never complained. Despite her exhaustion, she lay awake at night, touching her belly. She never thought about the future.

15.

Grete Anders returned to the village in September, when the trees had become tired and the mornings were slow to rise.

She arrived at around midday. By lunch at one o'clock, the entire village knew her business. There was not one kitchen where people were not gossiping about her, some with Schadenfreude, others regretfully. Everyone could see that the girl was in her fifth month at least, and old Anders had made such a song and dance about it that he could be heard houses away along the street.

Now the old man was standing in the parlour; in front of him stood Grete, her hands folded across her extended belly, looking at her grandfather with a calm, almost friendly expression. He was exhausted, his flaccid chin trembling, his anger having given way to deep fatigue. Lange was leaning against the wall and reasoning with him in a sympathetic, understanding voice, his scorn barely audible.

The old man propped himself on the table; he had to remain calm because his views on the matter didn't count for much, which he'd noticed as soon as Lange arrived, summoned by Grete. The young whippersnapper was now speaking to him, a man thirty years his senior, as if he were a naughty child.

'Think it over, Anders, think it over very carefully before you throw Grete out. She's carrying the child of an SS officer. Imagine, the SS . . . They're the crème de la crème, Anders, every woman ought to feel proud.'

I've heard this all before, thought the farmer. He didn't have to think very far back to July, when he'd run into Heinrich Marten, who'd ridden on his cart and said something similar. Drivel about 'honour', 'German women' and 'motherhood' fell on deaf ears in his case. He brooded. *This is the price I pay for blackening the name of Heinrich's wife in front of this know-it-all. Should've held my tongue, I didn't have any proof, I've only given Lange ammo. This is the payback . . .*

'To put it bluntly, Grete is staying in your house until the child is born.'

She doesn't even know whose it is, thought the old man. *What if the Marten girl really is carrying on with the Russian . . . But a dozen soldiers have had their paws on Grete – what's worse?*

He said sullenly, 'I won't put up with a whore under my roof. She should crawl back to the fellas she came from.'

Grete bit her lip, but her brown eyes remained blank. Lange lost his temper, and red flecks appeared on his cheeks.

'You don't know what you're saying, Anders! I speak in the name of the Party and I order—'

The old man perked up, thrusting his wrinkly chin out with a sudden roar: 'Out, you whore! Out, you bloody fool! She can throw her bastard out on the street and let the pigs she took to bed cough up for it.' The old man's reedy voice cracked. 'I don't give a shit about any of you! I'm not going to be ordered around, especially not by your Party! Pigs, all of you! Trampling everything into the dirt. Honour—' He spat out the word, and his bony face turned a blueish hue, then he gurgled something incomprehensible, choked with rage. The other two had already left.

That same evening, Anders was arrested. His granddaughter moved into his house with all her worldly possessions, and her many clothes including the muslin dress, as pink as candyfloss. But in all honesty, she couldn't wear it any more because she was too round.

Her mother didn't dare kick up a fuss. She cried a lot over her old father-in-law and never once asked her cheeky, self-assured daughter who the father of the child was. But sometimes she gave the girl a sidelong glance, and there was a baffled look in her tear-stained eyes: had she really given birth to this pretty, sassy, odd creature?

Anders came back about a week later. No one found out what had happened to him or why they'd let him go. He barely had any teeth left and now always wore a cap; his head was shaven, and a few dark-blue welts crisscrossed his scalp.

He was now older than ever. When he talked, he mumbled and couldn't stop his fingers from trembling. People said he was no longer quite right in the head; when he passed Grete, he bared his teeth at her and garbled gibberish.

The girl would then smile and walk past her uncontrollably shaking grandfather, in a calm, almost friendly way, her round belly thrust in front of her.

Red and blue asters bobbed on long stalks. The bush beans were already tall and would soon be ready for picking. Ripe pumpkins peeked out from under enormous leaves.

Kathrin was standing on the ladder. These days, she had to hold fast with one hand, as she quickly felt dizzy. She was picking apples, warm from the late summer sun; when you bit into them, they squirted sweet juice. Kathrin blinked through the branches. In another tree, crouching, half-hidden by boughs, was Alexei.

She climbed a few rungs higher and had to stretch to reach the remaining apples in the treetop.

Suddenly, she grabbed her chest and fell without a sound.

Alexei carried her into the house. She had no serious injuries, and a few days later her aches and pains had disappeared. But from then on, she suffered from panic attacks, no longer climbed ladders, barely dared go out and started at every sound.

Frieda didn't think anything of it. Young women were bound to go a bit peculiar when their husbands were away for a long time – it was just 'nerves', and they'd soon pass.

But for Alexei it was different. He watched Kathrin's every move, always kept close by and couldn't put the sight of her pale, grimacing face when he'd picked her up from under the apple tree out of his mind.

It grew hot again for two or three days. On the third day, towards evening, dark clouds gathered and, in the distance, thunder grumbled. Kathrin paced restlessly around the farm and house, an inexplicable anxiety rising in her. She watched the strange mountains of clouds towering in the sky, steely-blue with sulphurous-yellow edges as if the sun were setting behind an enormous mountain range.

She hoped the thunderstorm would pass while it was still light, but evening came, and then night, and the storm only approached slowly.

Kathrin lay in bed, worrying the lavender-smelling linen with her fingers and pressing herself into the pillows as she trembled. Squalls of wind howled around the house and flung sand at the windows, while lightning flickered brightly in the room at intervals.

Kathrin started when the first powerful crash of thunder broke, and her hand darted instinctively to her belly to protect her unborn child. Hail clattered drily, and the house shuddered. She thought she'd never been through such a terrible storm.

Suddenly gripped by fear, she jumped out of bed and raced down the stairs and out of the house, barely clothed. The storm seized her and hurled her against the wall, taking her breath away. With great effort, she groped her way forward and rattled at the barn door. It wasn't locked. Frieda had become lackadaisical; she'd become so used to the prisoner that she no longer thought he would run away.

Alexei pulled the sobbing woman towards him. He stroked her wet hair out of her face, and as she slowly calmed down in his arms, her heart hammered less wildly against her ribs.

They sat down next to each other in the hay. Kathrin listened out for the rain drumming on the barn roof. 'In the past, autumn used to make me sad,' she said. 'In the past, I thought I'd die very young.'

She was shaking with cold. Alexei wrapped her up

in his jacket and felt her neck and face, which were hot. 'You have a fever, Katyusha.'

'Because I was so alone . . .' After a while, she said, 'Do you know what I think? I used to think too much about death because I didn't know what I was living for. But now, autumn's beautiful – the sky seems much higher than in summer and bluer than in any other season. The church looks like it's on fire, and the vine leaves are all red . . .' She laughed shyly. 'Perhaps like the coat of the king in the fairytale, gold and purple . . .'

Alexei took hold of her hot hand and said uneasily, 'You seem so different today, Katja, my dove.'

She laughed again. 'I'm talking and talking . . . I suddenly feel like I have to tell you everything – about myself, the past, and when I saw you for the first time.'

The storm rattled at the barn door. Kathrin pressed her face into Alexei's chest and murmured, 'The rain's so beautiful, isn't it?'

'If you have a roof over your head,' said Alexei.

She kissed his neck and face. 'We'll always have a roof over our heads, Alyosha.'

They no longer heard the wind wrench open the door, which was only ajar, making it crash against the wall.

Frieda was tossing and turning in bed, unable to sleep. Such a wild night again! The shutters at her windows rattled dully. She must have forgotten to fasten them properly, and the storm might shatter the panes. Frieda didn't have the least desire to get up and close them now but then she remembered how the cows had broken loose during a gale the previous year, causing a fine mess in the cowshed when they'd panicked.

She listened out into the roaring storm. After all, she

was the one who carried all the responsibility. She had to get up and check on the cows. What was she supposed to tell Heinrich if something happened to the cattle?

The thought of Heinrich clinched it. Sighing, she rose heavily from her bed, threw on her skirt, lit the candle in the lantern and clopped, her bare feet in wooden clogs, through the kitchen and across the yard.

The cows were stamping restlessly in their stalls but they hadn't broken loose. Frieda came out of the cowshed, and her gaze fell on the barn. At that moment, an icy-cold shock went through her, right to her fingertips. The barn door was a dark rectangle, and the wind was playing with the door. The Russian! Escaped! Frieda clutched her chest, as a searing realization hit her – it was her fault! She'd forgotten to lock the barn. She jogged heavily back into the house, not able to think straight, only knowing that she now had to lock the door so that there was no proof of her blunder. The prisoner might be gone, but she wouldn't be the culprit – that was it!

The lantern swung in her hands, and Frieda could barely hold the key. She stole up to the door, thinking that perhaps he was asleep and hadn't noticed.

Inside all was quiet.

Frieda ventured another step. She raised her lantern, and the shaft of light flickered across two people lying in the hay, locked in a tight embrace, sleeping soundly, not as if all hell had broken loose outside but as if there were peace on earth.

Frieda's eyes hung on stalks. She stared, mesmerized, at the sleeping couple. Kathrin let out a sigh and pressed her head against the shoulder of the man in whose arms she lay.

Heinrich, thought Frieda.

That whore is lying here with the Russian while you're on the front being shot at!

I didn't pay attention; I didn't watch her every move. I should've realized long ago, Heinrich – how can I explain myself?

She was shaking all over. The storm was wailing in the trees. The lantern fell from her grip and to the floor, the glass shattering. The candle was snuffed out.

Alexei flinched and, for a few moments, saw her large frame in the door; then she disappeared, the door slammed shut, and the key grated in the lock.

Alexei hugged Kathrin. They had ten minutes, perhaps fifteen, before the others got here.

'Katyusha,' he whispered, 'don't cry, Katyusha. We knew it would end one day.'

'They'll beat you to death.'

'I'll be thinking of you until the end. Be brave! We've done nothing wrong.'

'I love you, Alexei, I love you – I can't live without you.'

This ripped his heart in two. He jumped up and ran to the door, threw himself against it and battered it with his fists until they were sore. This was the end. They'd seen it coming and hadn't believed it would happen. They'd believed their love was stronger than the devil breathing down their necks.

The others were already on their way.

They had five more minutes, certainly no more. Kathrin in the hands of those animals; Kathrin, interrogated by those bastards, sent to their camps – these thoughts filled Alexei with dark despair. They were sitting in a trap with no escape; Alexei knew every last dusty cranny of the barn – its walls and joists were all solid.

Kathrin began talking in a quiet, unnaturally high voice. 'Do you believe in miracles, Alyosha?'

'No, I don't think so.'

Kathrin shook her head. 'I don't mean the kind of miracles we heard about in church. Not the ones with the loaves and two fish that fed five thousand starving people.'

'There are no miracles, no gifts,' Alexei said. 'You have to sow grain for five thousand loaves. You have to sail out to sea and catch ten thousand fish for the starving. That's how it is.'

Kathrin shuddered slightly, and her eyes widened. 'But a miracle just for us both – I'm allowed to believe in that, aren't I . . .?'

She knelt in front of Alexei and cupped his face in both her hands. In the dark, she couldn't make out his features but she knew them so well that she'd never forget the tiniest detail. 'Alexei, my love,' she said, 'I came to you tonight to give you courage . . . I'm going to have a baby.'

He didn't move, thinking that he was dreaming. 'Is it true, Kathrin?' he said, in a strangled whisper. Kissing her hands, he said, 'Ach, *golubka, golubotshka*, my little dove . . .'

'It's true, I'm going to have your baby, and it'll live, Alyosha, and be tall and strong, and good like you.'

Kathrin kissed the tears on his face. 'I will make it, I will—'

Voices in the yard.

In an instant, the couple were on their feet.

Kathrin clung to Alexei, pain wrenching her chest. 'If they'd only left us a few more weeks – a few more days – a single day . . .'

The doors flew open, and in stormed a couple of farmers, with Lange in the lead. Alexei stood up straight, his arms wrapped protectively around Kathrin.

The men pulled them apart.

The Russian yelled and lashed out in all directions, and he was then thrown to the ground. Lange kicked him in the side. The Russian writhed without making a noise.

Someone bent Kathrin's arms behind her back. She collapsed to her knees, was yanked up and dragged through the doorway. She felt no pain and craned her neck backwards to catch a last glimpse of her lover.

He was held in a grip by Lange and two farmers. Blood was running down his face, and the skin on his cheekbones was grazed.

Kathrin gave a heart-rending scream.

Alexei shouted, 'Farewell, Katyusha!' A fist hit his jaw, and he spat blood.

Kathrin dug her fingers into the doorpost. She locked eyes with the blue-black eyes of her lover one last time, and a silent goodbye passed between them.

Then the night engulfed them.

16.

For three weeks after that, every day, Kathrin Marten was interrogated. She stood rigidly and stiffly in front of the men as if she were deranged and they couldn't get a word out of her. For hours, the blinding white lights from their lamps tormented her poor, confused mind.

She was beaten; once, an SS man dragged her by the hair all around the room. She didn't speak. This pale, slight woman was as tough as a willow switch and didn't break. The men might as well have tried to force a confession from the blank wall.

Her nights in the cell were filled with thoughts of Alexei; he was ever-present, and she brought his smile, his gaze and the squeeze of his hand into the interrogations. He talked to her, his voice drowning out the insults and curses of the men torturing her.

When they beat her, she only protected her belly. The child had to survive because it was part of Alexei, his flesh and blood.

For its sake, Kathrin wanted to live.

After three weeks, her sentence was passed. Kathrin wasn't afraid. She'd known her fate since the first time Alexei had kissed her.

Heinrich Marten was given special leave.

The disastrous news hadn't visibly rattled him; it only confirmed his grim suspicions. His letters hadn't been addressed to Kathrin for a long time, only to Frieda. The other woman, whom he sometimes still called his wife, wouldn't have read them anyway.

The house was so empty. What a sorry homecoming!

Brother and sister stood in the kitchen silently facing each other. Frieda was sobbing. Something held Heinrich back from putting his arms around her. The staircase creaked; he flinched and gave a sudden laugh, horrifying Frieda. His laughter sounded like someone was shaking a sack full of glass splinters.

'How on earth did it all come to this?' he asked.

'I don't know, I can't tell you, Heinrich.'

Frieda was so confused that she could barely talk in straight sentences. The day before yesterday, someone had thrown a stone the size of a fist through Lange's window, missing him by a whisker. Since then, Frieda had been terrified to be in the house, it was so deathly quiet, and had it been up to her, she'd have moved out. She was in over her head with all the work on the farm. Not only that but ever since the night of the storm, Trude Meinhardt had started walking past her on the street without saying hello.

'You fetched the others?' Heinrich asked.

'Yes, yes, I did . . .' Frieda wrung her hands, her knuckles standing out white against her ruddy skin. She swallowed. 'What was I supposed to do? If you'd seen the pair of them lying there – and you so far away . . .' Her head fell forward onto the table, and she started crying wildly and desperately.

'Did you have to?' he asked. His brown eyes stared, helpless and sullen.

'Heinrich, Heinrich,' sobbed the woman, 'you're all I

have in the world. Because of you, I never married. I've always taken care of you and kept the farm in order . . . I can't help what's happened.' She kept her eyes fixed on him, begging for a kind word.

'No, you can't help it,' he said. He left the kitchen and went to stand for a long time in the barn, which smelled sweetly and pungently of hay. He thought: *You shouldn't have done this, Kathrin. Not this. I didn't treat you badly. The only reason I hit you that one time was down to the bloody booze. I was always fond of you – why did you take another man? And why did you have to waste yourself on a Russian? You shouldn't have done this, Kathrin – things weren't that terrible with me.*

But deep in his heart, he knew that things had been terrible for her and that although he hadn't been bad to her, he hadn't been good to her either, had never understood or tried to understand her.

He went back into the house and asked Frieda, 'What kind of person was the Russian?' He referred to the man as if he were dead.

'Well, he was nice enough, you know, kept himself to himself – how should I put it? . . . nothing special at all.' As if to justify herself, she hastily added, 'She just wanted to jump into bed with someone, it didn't really matter who—'

Heinrich frowned and said sternly, 'No, Kathrin's not like that.' He mulled this over, then thought aloud: 'I must've done something wrong. She's not the kind to fling herself at just anyone. She was always so shy and tiny and when I was home in July, she'd let her hair grow and looked so pretty.'

Frieda groped for his hand. She seemed small and

cowed all of a sudden; nothing of bossy Frieda, or her strength and healthy glow remained. She'd seen the Russian's face covered in blood that night and had heard his last words – 'Farewell, Katyusha!' All this ate into her heart. When she closed her eyes, she saw the pair of them lying in the hay, holding each other tightly, Kathrin's head resting on the man's shoulder. That had been Frieda's dream as a young girl – to love and be loved, to feel looked after . . .

Brother and sister sat silently facing each other, an icy chill and a growing sense of guilt surrounding them.

17.

Monotonous drizzle fell, thin and cold.

The market square gleamed as if scrubbed clean, as the rain fell onto the round stones; the town was old, and the war was guzzling up its wealth, so the market was still covered in cobbles rather than asphalt.

Rows of people stood there, packed in tightly, like a thin grey wall surrounding the wooden podium, which towered nearly two metres over the square; from up high, Kathrin could see over the wall of people.

The dignified houses with heavily ornamented gables and window ledges looked down surly-faced on the marketplace, their façades blurry. The crowd had been waiting in silence for over an hour now. When the spectacle had begun, a few young hoodlums had caused a commotion. Now their taunts were drowned by the persistent rain, which slowly seeped into their clothing, touching their skin with sharp, cold fingers.

The woman was sitting on a wooden chair like a frozen image. Dripping wet, her grey apron clung to her gaunt limbs. Her eyes stared without seeing. She was forced to let her arms hang by her sides because a broad, white sign on her chest said: 'I AM A RUSSIAN WHORE!'

Dry-eyed, she'd read the block capital letters that morning as the sign was being hung around her neck; she was already beyond feeling shame.

Monotonous drizzle fell, thin and cold.

Kathrin's frozen face gazed straight ahead. But beneath the mask her thoughts were teeming. Many things went through her mind during those hours, both good and bad. She weighed the first twenty-eight years of her life against the past half a year, and realized that it had much more weight.

Astonished, Kathrin thought: *Why was I afraid of the pillory?*

These people are standing down there, getting wet but not leaving, just staring at me. Maybe three of them hate me. Maybe thirty of them despise me. Maybe one of them pities me. They're standing there and staring at me because I loved someone. It's so hard to understand. They love people too, all of them, men, women and children. When this is all over, they'll go home to warmth and love. They'll kiss and sleep with each other and maybe a couple of them will think of me and laugh or cry. Everything will be just like it was before.

No, nothing would ever be like it was before. In that hour of deepest humiliation, an insight came and took hold of the dishonoured woman, filling her mind and heart: when this was all over and she had climbed down from the podium, the world would have moved on a tiny step.

A man stepped up behind her chair, scissors in hand.

Kathrin heard the dull thud of his footfall on the wooden planks and at that moment she saw a face before her: the sky blazed bloodily, reflecting the fiery glow of burning cities, and people in their hundreds and thousands – burned, beaten, tortured – fell onto trampled crops, a heap of corpses piling high until it reached the sky. The world drowned in fumes and blood, and darkness fell.

Kathrin closed her eyes.

A ray of light fought against the darkness, and thundering footsteps threatened to tear the sky apart. A man stepped out of the wall of mist. Wherever he looked, it became light and wherever he trod, grass and flowers sprang to life.

Then Kathrin knew: we've finally achieved what people have died for, thousands of years long. Her heart burned in her chest like a flame. She recognized the man – it was Alexei, his silhouette, his kind, strong face. Smiling, he reached his hands out towards her. 'Kathrin!' he called, and his voice echoed back from the heavens.

'Alexei!' she called out. The cold steel touched her head, a few rowdies began to jeer, and a high-pitched woman's voice rose from the grey crowd as her lovely blonde hair fell to the ground, one shank at a time.

Kathrin opened her eyes and saw the heads swaying down below like ears of corn in the wind; she could hear a surge of excited chatter. A man abruptly turned away and crossed the street. Kathrin recognized his broad back. A long time ago, she had lived with a man called Heinrich Marten. Kathrin saw him now in piercing detail; he was veering like a drunkard. She also spotted a pale, grave face framed by ebony hair that belonged to a woman called Trude Meinhardt. She lifted her hands against the pillory, tears running down her cheeks.

A man led Trude aside, and then she crouched on the kerb in the rain, her head buried in her arms, thinking: *God forgive me but I would have given the life of my second son to stop this.*

Kathrin's hair was scattered, wet and dirty, across the wooden podium. The rain whipped against her bare skull, and she clutched at her head with both hands. Down below, a woman laughed shrilly. Kathrin's arms fell back down as if she'd been shot.

It was like a signal. Suddenly a stone was flung at Kathrin's shoulder. A second followed, then a third. She flinched. The SS men at the back yelled, as if chanting 'Get her! Get her!' to the crowd. A girl hurled handfuls of dirt at the podium like a madwoman, and someone called out 'Ugh!' but whether it referred to the girl or the woman in the pillory, no one knew.

But most people stood there mutely, filled with disgust and horror. A few years earlier, when a Jewish girl had been put in the stocks, they'd shouted in unison and had thrown stones; but four years of war had deadened them, and the inflammatory cries of the watchmen found no echo.

A last stone fell with a clatter to the wooden floor. It was only a small pebble, but it would smash to pieces the life of the person who threw it.

Liesel Weckerling trembled when she saw the glare of the man by her side. 'Paul,' she whispered. He raised his hand, and Liesel ducked. He said, 'Don't worry, I'll not dirty my hands on you.' Then he turned and left.

The wall of people started to crumble, the gaps between people growing bigger and bigger as they drifted away. Almost all of them were peaceful citizens who would have been embarrassed to publicly jeer at the woman in the pillory. But the spectacle had enticed them, albeit only at the start when they'd been waiting for something that didn't happen, even though they couldn't say what.

Now they felt uneasy. They'd imagined whores differently, not still and pale like the woman with the shaved head, sallow and skull-like.

'Poor thing, still so young,' said a man quietly, then glanced around in shock, hoping that no one had heard him; after all, she'd messed about with a Russian.

Kathrin was led from the podium down the small staircase. On the last step, she was forced to stop. A girl was thrusting her way through the thinning crowd, one of the last gawkers; she had brown eyes, a snub nose and a protruding belly.

Kathrin recognized Grete Anders.

The girl leaned back her head, then hurled herself forward and spat right into Kathrin's face.

Kathrin reeled. An officer gave a raucous laugh. She grabbed her chest, and a wave ran through her as if a tiny finger were writing mysterious signs inside.

She wiped the spit from her face. She looked at the other woman and saw that she was pregnant.

Kathrin smiled.

Then she was led away.

18.

Kathrin had a cold and was feverish.

When the cell door opened, she stayed lying down with one hand pressed against her burning forehead.

'Kathrin!' the man called out hoarsely. He was standing by the door as if nailed to the spot. Though he'd never been inside a prison, it was all exactly like he'd imagined as a boy: the grey walls covered in scratches, the pail in the corner, the bunk and the barred window framing a tiny piece of sky thick with rainclouds.

Heinrich shuddered in the damp, cool air. 'I just wanted to see you one last time, Kathrin!' he said. *There was so much I wanted to say but now I've forgotten it all. At least look at me . . .* he thought.

The woman lifted her shaven head; she looked even worse than he'd feared. Red, blotchy circles scorched her cheeks. 'Are you sick?' Heinrich asked. Then he didn't know what to do. Ten minutes, that was all he had, and it felt unreal. Ten more minutes with the woman he'd lived with for five years and when it was over, he'd walk out and never see her again.

'Why did you do it, Kathrin?' he murmured.

Kathrin didn't think there was any point in talking to him about her love, and about how kind, clever and brave Alexei was. But she said anyway, 'You make it sound like a crime. But how can it be a crime to love someone so much that you're not afraid of anything in the world?

Before that, I wasn't living a real life – I didn't even know why I'd been born. I didn't think about it. I just accepted it, like it was sent from above.'

Heinrich only vaguely understood what the horribly transfigured woman was talking about. He moved hesitantly away from the cell door and came over to her bunk, seeming bigger and heavier in the square of darkness. He bent over Kathrin and looked into her grey face: she looked haggard and feverish, and two deep lines cut its gentle oval shape in two.

She won't last much longer, he thought, *she looks so ill. What has she got to live for?* As if she'd guessed what he was thinking, Kathrin said, 'I don't want to die, Heinrich. This can't be how my life ends, especially now that it has meaning, with dreams and a goal.' She smiled, and her eyes gleamed, which Heinrich thought was because of her fever.

He gingerly sat at the foot of the bunk, and it creaked under his weight. He said, 'You had such lovely hair.'

He was startled by his own words. Was that all that was left to say? He suddenly realized that time was racing by and he only had a few minutes left; he had to hurry because there was so much he still wanted to know. Hurriedly, he asked, 'When you did it, Kathrin, didn't you think of me at all?'

For the first time, Kathrin pulled herself up, leaning on her elbows and said, clearly and harshly, 'Yes, Heinrich I did. I hated you, from the day you wrote to me that you'd shot women and children. From then on, I knew we didn't belong to each other any more.'

Heinrich flared up, his eyes bulging, and the old tone returned to his voice as he shouted, 'You don't know what you're talking about, Kathrin! We know why we have to use such harsh measures! And anyway, orders are orders!'

'Ah, yes,' Kathrin said. 'You wrote that too: "Orders are orders." Are you saying you all knew why you were gunning down women and children? No, you don't know!' she cried. 'You just carry out orders given by madmen. You've become animals because animals give you orders.'

'You've gone insane,' he gasped. He heaved himself up, stood with his legs apart and thrashed the air with both hands. 'That's – that's pure treason! If I report it—' His bulky body, tense with indignation just a moment before, slumped. His wife gave him a gentle, mocking smile. 'See, Heinrich,' she said in a friendly tone, 'there's no point in doing that. I'm already in prison.'

Heinrich walked over to the window. It was too high for him to reach and the square piece of sky was sharply dissected by the bars.

He heard Kathrin's voice behind him. 'Once you were a farmer, Heinrich. You tilled the earth, fed the cattle and didn't think about killing. I still remember that you hated slaughtering the chickens. You did it, but not gladly, I can remember that very clearly. And now? How come you can shoot people now? They've done you no harm, they're no different to the people in our village, Liesel or Trude Meinhardt and her boy, and all the others. Why don't your hands shake with fear when you point your gun at them?'

Heinrich murmured, 'I'm sorry when I do it. Do you really think it's so easy for me?' He turned around and said loudly and hurriedly, 'But what am I supposed to do? The others do it too, and if I refuse, I'll be shot. That wouldn't make anything better, you have to understand that.'

The hinges of the cell door screeched. 'Time's up!'

'I have to go now.' He hesitantly stretched his hand out to Kathrin. 'Goodbye, then, Kathrin.' He knew he would never see her again. He'd heard that she was going to be sent to a women's camp.

Kathrin pulled his head down towards her. Very close to his ear, she breathed, 'It's never too late to change, Heinrich. We have so much to make up for.'

'Kathrin,' Heinrich stammered.

The uniformed prison guard rattled her keys. 'Time's up now!' she shouted sharply.

He left, pausing at the door for a moment and staring back at the grey bundle lying crooked on the bunk. 'Well – all the best,' he forced out, and was about to add something, then shook his head heavily before trudging off like a tired, very old man.

The iron steps clanged under his feet, and he thought: *She's all alone now. Strange, I'm not angry with her at all. Even though she cheated on me, and with a Russian . . .*

As he marched along the town's streets, his gaze on the wet cobblestones, he tried to work up a rage. Yes, indeed, she'd cheated on him, she'd flung herself at a Russian! He tried to picture the two of them lying together – but he couldn't. Over and over, the image of the shorn woman with red blotches on her haggard cheeks got in the way, and he caught himself thinking that the Russki must have been quite some fellow for shy Kathrin to have fallen in love with him.

And he had cheated on her with quite a few women.

He sat down in a pub, lost in thought as he stared into

his glass. In that hour, Kathrin's last words rattled the mainstays of his robust life and lazy outlook. If only he could have shoved it all very far away – over, finished, done with, now for something new. But he couldn't. He tipped back glass after glass of strong-tasting schnapps to snuff out the picture of his wife. He threw coin after coin into the slot machine, but the tinkling sound couldn't drown out Kathrin's whispered words: 'It's never too late to change. We have so much to make up for.'

It was late by the time he went home. The sky was clear and starry again.

He stood in front of his farm and could have just as easily walked past.

Frieda had been waiting for her brother. She was startled when she saw him, his black hair hanging messily across his face and his eyes all red. He swayed and had to hold on tight to the doorpost.

Frieda grabbed his arm. 'You're drunk, Heinrich—'

He nodded. 'Indeed, I am. Drunk. That's right.' He yelled, 'What's a man supposed to do? What else have I got in this shitty life!'

'You shouldn't have gone into town,' whispered Frieda.

Heinrich fell off the kitchen chair. From below, he looked up at his sister, his dull eyes beginning to glint and his breathing coming heavily. Very slowly, he said, 'So, I shouldn't have gone. I shouldn't have taken a look at the damage you did.' Redemption was beckoning: Frieda was to blame for the abominable things that had happened. She'd reported the pair of them. 'You couldn't run to Lange fast enough. Why didn't you speak to Kathrin first? You knew they had it coming to them if they were caught.' His voice was thin and reedy, and he yanked open the top of his shirt. 'You knew exactly what you were doing – you informer!'

Frieda gave a heart-rending screech.

'It's all your fault – you—'

'Heinrich, Heinrich,' she whimpered, 'come to your senses! I did it for you because I love you and you know that – I couldn't just sit back and watch the pair of them carrying on, with you out in the field. I only wanted the best for you.' She threw her apron up to cover her face.

Heinrich jumped to his feet, and the chair clattered loudly onto the tiles. Swaying, he stood in front of his sister, balling his fist at her. 'You have her on your conscience. Don't make excuses! I don't want to see you here any more, I can't stand the sight of you – go, go, I say – go, before I lose control—'

Frieda fell awkwardly to her knees, then slid across the floor to her brother and put her arms around his legs.

'Heinrich,' she screeched, 'don't do this to me! I don't want to leave – where am I supposed to go? I have no one except you.'

He kicked her away with his foot. In doing so, he nearly lost his balance and that enraged him even more. 'Out!' he bawled. 'Out!' He went berserk, going blue in the face; he had to shout loud enough to drown out the voice that judged him equally guilty of Kathrin's fate.

Frieda struggled to her feet with unspeakable effort. Madness flickered in her wide, staring eyes, and her round face was distorted in horror. She went without saying a word, setting one foot in front of the other like a sleepwalker, out of the kitchen, out of the house, across the yard, onto the street, then down to the fields.

On his own, Heinrich shivered and looked around.

The walls were plastered with thousands of white faces with round, red holes in their foreheads. They stared at him silently. In desperation, he shouted back at the faces, 'I'm innocent! I – am – innocent!'

A dread came over him. He sank forward on the table, his powerful shoulders quivering, and murmured, 'Am I innocent? Just answer me—'

19.

The following day, Frieda Marten's body was hauled out of the lake.

Heinrich had personally asked the farmers to trawl the lake, and no one had refused to help.

Water ran from the woman's hair, and soon she was lying in a cloudy puddle. Sullenly, Heinrich watched as the men laid his sister on a stretcher and carried her home. He couldn't even feel grief.

That same evening, he went back to the front. His heart was still beating, his eyes could still see, and his legs could still carry him. He could also move his arms and speak and hear what was said to him. But the life had gone out of him, and he knew he wouldn't return.

Not even two weeks later, he was hit by a partisan's bullet. It went clean through his lung. He might have pulled through but he had no will left to nurture the weak flame of life; so he quickly died.

At almost the same time, a truck crammed with female prisoners rattled through the gates of a women's concentration camp. Among them was Kathrin Marten.

Kathrin Marten lived – if that hellish existence could be called 'life'.

She was able to keep her pregnancy secret for long enough to prevent her child being taken away. She worked like the other women, was beaten like the other women and sank, deathly tired, onto her hard bunk in the evening like the other women. She learned from them – they were real political activists – and inside that barbed-wire compound, her world expanded.

On the whole, she suffered no more and no less than the thousands of women in the camp; but it was enough to make dull animals out of angels – and enough for anyone who'd lost faith or who had no good reason to stay alive.

When Kathrin gave birth to her child, she was just a heap of skin and bones, held together by abject will. That was in early April 1944.

She was in her late twenties and had never given birth before; her weakened body was torn apart by the pain. She bit into her arm so as not to cry out. The child was a boy, puny with bony limbs, but he had the round head and wide-set, deep-blue eyes of his father. That's why Kathrin believed he would pull through and grow up strong like Alexei.

Alexei Ivanovich Luniev died in spring 1944 in Buchenwald concentration camp, together with hundreds of Soviet prisoners of war. As he knelt at the edge of the grave he'd dug for himself and was kicked into it by the SS officer behind him, Alexei thought that Katyusha must have given birth by now and very much hoped that it was a boy. Then he fell forward, his skull smashed.

A year later, the inmates of the women's concentration camp were liberated by the Allies.

Kathrin Marten, her child in arm, walked down the familiar yet unfamiliar street of her village. It had come under artillery fire for some time, and most of the farms had been destroyed and burned to the ground. The residents had fled, God knows where to, and the empty window sockets gaped horribly.

On the corner where the inn had once stood, Kathrin came across the past. She almost didn't recognize Trude Meinhardt because her black hair had gone completely grey and she didn't hold herself as straight as she used to.

Trude showed no surprise. She just said, 'You're back, Kathrin.'

She lifted the sleeping child from Kathrin's arms. She asked, 'This is Alexei, isn't it?'

Kathrin nodded and with two fingers she stroked the boy's round head, where short blond hair was starting to curl like fluff on a young bird. When she lifted her arm, her jacket sleeve slipped down, and Trude saw the number tattooed on her waxy pale skin. She swallowed.

'So much has changed,' she said. 'We've all changed. So many have died. My boy was called up at the last minute to serve in the Air Force Auxiliary. He was fifteen years old. I don't even know where he's buried. What will you do now?'

'I'll go to the farm,' said Kathrin.

Trude thought about this. 'It's still there, but it's a sight. There aren't any cattle left.'

'We have to start all over again,' said Kathrin.